Wish upon a Star

Other Avalon Books by Karen Morrell

FOR THE LOVE OF LAURA

*W*ISH *upon a* STAR
Karen Morrell

Fic
More

AVALON BOOKS
THOMAS BOUREGY AND COMPANY, INC.
401 LAFAYETTE STREET
NEW YORK, NEW YORK 10003

PRINTED IN THE UNITED STATES OF AMERICA
ON ACID-FREE PAPER
BY HADDON CRAFTSMEN, SCRANTON, PENNSYLVANIA

This book is dedicated to my generous sister, Linda Bailey, for helping me with the research. Thank you for treating me to the cruise. I love you, little doc.

And, to Ruth and Herschel Black for their inspiration and memories. May all your wishes come true.

Chapter One

The front door of Sadie's Place burst open, letting in a blast of frigid December air and a hunched-over creature so snow-covered that the three women behind the counter stopped talking and stared openly.

"Reg . . . register . . . registered let . . . letter for Annie Stewart," the voice from beneath the hood stuttered.

"That you, Gus?" Sadie McKracken asked, scurrying across the black-and-white tile floor to get a closer look.

"It's me," the muffled voice replied while a gloved hand wiped ice from his mustache. Dribbles of slush slid from his rubber boots onto the well-worn floor. "It's colder than an Eskimo's eyelashes out there."

Gus toppled into an end booth, his mail pouch weighing him down considerably. Annie Stewart, Sadie's head waitress, poured him a cup of steaming coffee while Diane, a part-time high school student, set his standard order, a warm slice of apple pie, on the table in front of him.

Annie watched as Gus slid the bulging bag from his shoulder, her mind blank for a moment. Then she re-

1

alized what he had said. "Did you say I had a registered letter?" she asked, certain she had misunderstood.

Gus slurped his coffee and nodded.

"Somebody's probably been trying to call you and finally gave up," the grill cook, Elmo, remarked from the nearby kitchen.

"It ain't Annie's fault that her good-for-nothin' brother ran up the phone bill while he was datin' that girl from Des Moines. It ain't her fault the phone company pulled the plug," Sadie said in her gravelly voice. "Now hush up, Elmo, so we can hear what this is all about."

Gus produced an envelope from the breast pocket of his coat. "You gotta sign for it, then it's all yours, Annie."

"Ain't you gonna make her show three pieces of identification with her picture on it?" Elmo jeered.

Gus laughed. "I've known Annie since the day I put her birth certificate into her mother's mailbox, God rest her soul, some twenty-three years ago."

"Twenty-four," Annie corrected. She hurriedly wrote her signature and reached for the letter.

Four pairs of eyes stared at her as she broke the seal of the heavy tan envelope and tugged out the contents. She held her breath and her heart stopped. Her hands began to tremble before she'd finished reading the first sentence. "I can't believe it," she whispered, her eyes scanning the page.

Sadie, who was too short to read over Annie's shoulder, peered around her employee's elbow. "Spill the news, girl. I've got a basket of fries poppin' to get out of the fat."

Annie looked up and smiled. "I won a trip! An incredible trip!" she said, hugging her waist and giving herself a twirl. She felt as if she could float to the ceiling. She read the letter again to make sure that there were no mistakes and that it was really meant for her. Life was full of disappointments, and she didn't need one more.

"Ain't you gonna tell us where you're gonna go?" Elmo was out of the kitchen now and standing between Diane and Sadie.

"Of course she is," Sadie interjected. She gave Annie a knowing look.

As Annie read the letter for a third time and confirmed that she was indeed the winner, a mischievous grin tugged at the corners of her mouth. Exciting events were few and far between at Sadie's Place and she wanted to prolong the sense of expectation for as long as she could. She carefully folded and tucked the pages back into the envelope, then slid it into her apron pocket. "It won't be long before the dinner crowd starts rolling in. I'd better get those setups finished." The impish expression on her face belied her nonchalant air.

"Did you win one of those contests you're always enterin'?" Sadie pressed on.

"That's right," Annie replied while meticulously placing a spoon, knife, and fork in the middle of a white paper napkin. "I never dreamed I'd win anything like this!"

Gus snorted. "At least I won't have to deliver this one. That microwave you won a couple of summers ago near tore my back out trying to get it through the door of your trailer.''

''Oh, Gus, quit your complainin' so the girl can speak,'' Sadie said. ''Are you going to Hollywood so you can try out for that game show you've got all figured out?''

Annie tossed another roll of cutlery onto the pile. ''Even better than that! I just can't believe it! I'm going—''

Before she could finish, two burly truckers burst through the door. ''There's an eighteen wheeler overturned on the guardrail about a mile back on I–80, Sadie,'' one man exclaimed as he made his way to a table. ''Looks like nobody's hurt, but it's going to shut down the highway for a couple of hours.''

''The ice is getting slicker by the minute,'' the other man said, shrugging off his heavy wool coat. ''We just booked into Hazel's for the night. I imagine within the hour this little diner's going to be bursting at the seams.''

Sadie threw her arms into the air. ''Land's sake, if this ain't a day and a half. First Annie, now this.'' She shot off toward the kitchen, mumbling, ''I hope there's enough veal cutlets in the freezer.''

''What's up with you, Annie?'' one of the truckers asked.

''I'll tell you in a minute,'' Annie said with a smile. ''But first I'll bring you some cinnamon buns. Elmo just took them from the oven.''

''Bring one for yourself and sit a spell,'' Gus called after her. ''Once the crowd hits, you won't get a break till midnight.''

Annie knew that Gus was right. But the thought of extra work didn't bother her at all. She enjoyed working at Sadie's, although she didn't want to spend the rest of her life waiting tables. She envied the freedom of the truckers and dreamed of someday traveling to every state. But that was later and this was now.

She hastened back to the dining area, set a basket of warm rolls and some butter on the table, efficiently poured mugs of coffee, and handed out menus. Gus had joined the truckers at their table, and Annie sat down in the fourth chrome-and-vinyl chair. She adjusted the pink satin bow around the long, thick, tawny braid at the nape of her neck.

"Confound it, Annie," Gus complained. "Are you going to keep us hangin' on a string all afternoon?"

Annie buttered a roll for herself. She knew if she didn't reveal the details soon, she'd be too giddy to work. Yet, deep inside, she wanted to savor the moment. Feelings of elation were all too infrequent for her.

She drew in a deep breath and let it out slowly. "Early last summer," she began, carefully measuring each word, "I entered a jingle contest for the Toasty Oatsy Cereal Company. My entry won the grand prize. And that prize is"—she turned to make sure Sadie's head was sticking through the pickup window before continuing—"an all-expenses-paid Christmas cruise to the Caribbean."

"If that doesn't beat all," Gus said, shaking his gray head. "Even better than the microwave."

"There's more," Annie said with an expression of sheer delight on her face. "Before the cruise I'll spend two days in Miami on a shopping spree, and at each port I'll get 'a fabulous Christmas present valued at over one thousand dollars,' " she read from the letter, now clutched in her hands.

"A Christmas cruise!" Sadie exclaimed, making her way around the tables while juggling several boxes in her arms. "That's only three weeks away!"

Annie nodded sheepishly. "I know. The letter says they tried to phone me."

"I knew it," Elmo yelled from the kitchen.

"Do you think you could get by without me for a week or so?" Annie asked Sadie, who was now refilling the candy and gum boxes beside the cash register.

Sadie gave a throaty chuckle. "I can't remember you askin' for a day off in six years. I guess I could get by with ten or fifteen high-school girls to take your place."

"Some of my friends would love the extra money for Christmas," Diane chimed in.

"Then it's settled," Sadie said with a decisive nod.

Annie winked at the petite, leprechaunlike woman whom she had grown to love and respect over the years. Sadie McKracken was the most courageous, kind, and generous woman Annie knew. The sixty-two-year-old red-haired dynamo had singlehandedly managed the restaurant for almost a quarter of a century after her husband was killed in Vietnam. And, Annie mused, regardless of how insurmountable a task might seem, Sadie was not one to give up easily. She could be very stubborn when she set her mind to something, a trait Annie shared.

"You'll have to watch out for all the rich men on that cruise," Sadie instructed, breaking into her thoughts. "I don't know if you realize just how conniving those old wolves can be."

Disbelievingly, Annie leaped to her feet. "Sadie! Really!" she protested. Dealing with truckers was as much a part of her daily routine as making coffee.

"Some millionaire playboy will probably come along and sweep you off your feet," Gus taunted.

"Don't count on it," she said with conviction. A small furrow formed between her honey-blond brows. "I can barely handle taking care of Rick. The last thing I need right now is another man to pick up after."

Gus snorted. "Your brother is an overgrown juvenile delinquent. You should have tossed him out on his ear two years ago when he turned eighteen."

Annie walked behind the counter and put a new filter in the ancient coffee maker. "I promised Mom I'd make sure Rick finished technical school. He's supposed to graduate in May." She hoped he'd make it. She hadn't given up on her own dream of going to college.

"Then he'll probably get married to Paula Davis," Diane added from behind the cash register. "At least that's what Paula keeps telling everyone at school."

Annie groaned inwardly and rolled her eyes toward the ceiling. The thought of her irresponsible half-brother marrying was preposterous. He couldn't even keep up the payments on his used car. He had no money sense whatsoever and bounced around from job to job faster than a cue ball on a pool table.

She sighed as she poured water into the seemingly

bottomless cylinder. It was hard to keep from worrying about Rick. For as long as she could remember she'd been trying to steer him away from trouble. Since his father had walked out before Rick entered grade school and their mother was dead, Annie felt responsible for him.

She briefly regarded her distorted reflection in the chrome coffee maker. She was hardly a woman men would go out of their way to pursue. Several loose, limp strands of blond hair surrounded her heart-shaped face. A band of freckles danced across her slightly upturned nose. And the lipstick that she'd applied at four-thirty that morning had long since worn off, she noticed. She flipped the switch to "brew."

The door swished open and several more customers entered. Annie rapidly filled water glasses. The dull thudding of the aged water pipes overhead pulsed in rhythm with her throbbing temples.

Elmo flipped a burger onto the sizzling griddle and called to her, "I hear the food on those ships is out of this world."

Sadie lugged a box from the meat locker and commented, "I bet there's a casino on board. Maybe you'll win a fortune."

"More like lose one," Gus said dryly.

Annie was oblivious to the chatter. She had a job to do. The trucker's prediction had been right. Sadie's Place soon filled to maximum capacity with tired, frazzled drivers and travelers. Voices rose and fell over the clink of dishes and silverware—noise overlaid with deep, smooth country songs flowing from the jukebox and jarring air horns blasting from the parking lot.

Savory smells of hamburgers and grilled onions and freshly baked cherry cobbler drifted from the kitchen. A veil of blue smoke hovered over tables weighed down with the heavy elbows of poker-playing truckers.

Annie went about her job with practiced efficiency. She piled a stack of dirty dishes and pushed them to one side, then wiped the shiny gray tabletop. With a last quick move, she emptied the ashtray onto a saucer that topped the stack.

"Be right with you," she called with a smile to a new arrival. As afternoon turned into evening, instead of giving into the cramping muscles in her calves, she actually had a spring in her step. Even her headache had vanished. The extent of the adventure she was about to embark on had firmly settled in her mind. She felt a mounting excitement bubble up inside her.

As she pocketed a meager tip, her mind rejoiced, *all expenses paid*. When a child sloshed his chocolate milk on the front of her crisply starched pink blouse, her heart sang, *a new wardrobe*. While she waited for Elmo to remove pickles and lettuce from a ham sandwich and add them to a roast beef, her inner self echoed, *fabulous Christmas presents*.

She maneuvered her way around the crowded tables, reveling in the thought that for seven glorious days she would have the freedom to step back from reality and live her greatest fantasy. She would no longer be plain, poor Annie Stewart, truck-stop waitress from Parker Junction, Iowa. Instead, she would be Anna. Poised. Advantaged. Liberated. She'd have the chance to wear glamorous clothes and jewelry, and have her hair done in a salon. She glanced at her hands, grasping the handles on both sides of a heavily laden tray, and a secret smile lit her face. She'd have her nails done, too, with deep crimson polish.

The vacation of her dreams. And during the week of Christmas—the timing couldn't have been more perfect. She had no family to share the holiday season with. Rick had already informed her that he'd planned to celebrate with his girlfriend.

Even as a child, Annie had never believed in Santa Claus. There was never enough money for a real tree or decorations or gifts. Until five years ago she'd usually received something practical from her mother, such as a sweater or a pair of gloves. Her brother never bothered with presents. Sometimes she treated herself to a canister of gourmet tea or a bag of potpourri. Last year Sadie had embroidered a scarf with Annie's initials on it. But this year she would have the celebration of a lifetime.

While she waited patiently for an elderly woman to decide whether to try the omelet or Sadie's specialty, veal cutlets, Annie absently watched a rivulet of moisture stream down the windowpane. Frost had formed in the corner, creating an intricate star-burst pattern. Laughter rose from a nearby table and the lilting sound of a mother and child singing "Jingle Bells" drifted over the booth behind her. Annie smiled, wondering if maybe, just maybe, there really was a Santa Claus.

Chapter Two

Phillipe Nadeau stood in the shadows of the Lido deck beside a towering stack of lounge chairs and watched a sleek, white limo pull up to the terminal. He leaned forward as a pair of long, shapely legs emerged. Giving a little nod, he smiled appreciatively at the stunning woman who emerged.

She was taller than average, Phillipe noted, perhaps five foot eight or nine. He leaned against the polished brass railing and continued to watch her out of idle curiosity. He had the casual stance of a man who didn't seem concerned that in an hour he'd be standing on center stage entertaining several hundred tourists.

The young woman gracefully descended the cement steps leading to the dock. Her shoulder-length hair was loose and waved gently, full and luxurious, with a wisp of bangs over her high forehead. It was the color of honey and shimmered with glints of gold in the midday sun.

Phillipe caught his breath when she extended her arms, gave a little twirl, and, smiling, lifted her face toward the sunshine. The expression of pure merriment, intended for no one else, piqued his interest.

He wondered if she was as charming as she appeared, or if it was just wishful thinking on his part. She was, Phillipe concluded, watching her fairly skip up the gangway, a creature of contrasts. She seemed to exude youthful energy and an open enthusiasm for life, yet dressed with the sophistication of a privileged background. In his experience, the two traits were incompatible.

Phillipe lost sight of her as she walked onto the ship. He stood, puzzled by the feeling that the sun had suddenly slipped behind a cloud.

"Enjoying the view?"

He turned around to discover a lifelong acquaintance approaching him. "Blake Emerson! It's good to see you!" he exclaimed, shaking his friend's extended hand. "I wondered if you'd make it on board before we set sail."

The trim, silver-haired man laughed. "Spoken like a true landlubber. I've been in the operations center since early this morning. It's almost time for me to make an appearance on the bridge."

It was Phillipe's turn to laugh. "As a passenger on this floating hotel, I can't think of a better place for the ship's captain. I understand we're booked to capacity."

Blake nodded and smiled. "Since you're the major stockholder for the cruise line, I'm sure you'll be delighted to know we have one thousand nine hundred and ninety-nine paying passengers for our maiden voyage."

Phillipe's brows rose. "And what about the two-thousandth guest?" he wanted to know.

The captain glanced at his watch. "If you'd care to come with me up to the bridge, I'll tell you all about her."

"Her?"

"I thought that would get your attention," Blake said, winking. As they crossed the deck and climbed a flight of stairs, he continued. "It seems we have a special woman on board. Her name is Annie Stewart. She's a waitress from Iowa."

"What makes her so special?"

"Miss Stewart is a clever young woman, my friend. So clever in fact that she wrote a jingle for a cereal company that's currently being sung in commercials nationwide. This cruise is her prize."

Phillipe ducked his head as he followed the captain through a passageway and down a narrow corridor. "A waitress, you say?"

Blake nodded. "From what I understand, this is the first time she's ever left the state of Iowa."

"You're joking!"

"On the contrary. Apparently she's somewhat disadvantaged. The company sponsoring her trip told me she doesn't even have a telephone."

Phillipe expelled a puff of air. "Is she traveling with anyone?"

The captain shook his head.

"Have you met her?" Phillipe asked.

"No. She wasn't among the first few hundred to arrive, and I've been so busy I haven't had a chance to check on her. If you meet her, extend a warm welcome on behalf of the ship."

Phillipe cleared his throat. "That reminds me of something I've been meaning to discuss with you."

Blake turned to face his friend. "Yes?"

"You're the only person, besides the board of directors, of course, who knows about my financial involvement with Tropicana Cruise Line. I'd like to keep it that way."

"Your secret's safe with me," Blake replied.

Phillipe smiled. "Do you have plans for dinner?"

The captain stopped at the door to the operations center. "As a matter of fact, I do. Since it's Christmas, my wife and stepdaughter are on board and I have something special lined up for them. Why don't you join us tomorrow night, about eight?" he offered.

Phillipe patted his friend on the shoulder. "Perfect." He peeked through the glass door and gave Blake a skeptical look. "Do you really know how to steer this thing?"

Blake shrugged. "Only time will tell."

"I think I'll go find a life preserver," Phillipe said, leaving the captain to his crew.

He headed back to his stateroom and passed the calypso band assembled near the pool. Their Spanish version of "Jingle Bells" drew cheers and laughter from the small crowd surrounding them, but the holiday song only served to remind Phillipe of the *real* reason he had decided to entertain on the holiday voyage. He wasn't here merely to determine if his money had been wisely invested. The truth was, it was Christmas and he was alone.

He shoved his hands into his pants pockets as he walked, his head downcast. Lately, he'd felt more tense and frustrated than he had in years. He was wealthy and successful beyond his greatest expectations. He'd had more platinum albums than anyone else in the recording industry. Yet he felt unfulfilled. Hollow inside. Empty.

He frowned as he negotiated his way around a heaping pile of luggage in the hallway, blaming his mood on the season, immersing himself in the knowledge that he was here to entertain. And entertain he would.

Annie balanced on tiptoe while she waited with several other passengers to enter the lounge. She watched a darkly handsome man who stood just inside the door chatting with several people. They seemed to swarm all over him. *Who on earth is that man?* she thought. He was a head taller than everyone else. But it wasn't only his six feet plus of height that caused him to stand out. As he flashed a dazzling smile at a trio of elderly women, she observed his expression of smug self-confidence, the kind that comes with knowing you're at the top of the heap. Like a cocky trucker who owned his own rig and let everyone else know it. But her gaze lingered on that smile.

When she stepped across the threshold into the room, he gave her a disarming smile. *"Bonsoir, mademoiselle,"* he said, placing a hand on her forearm. His touch was soft and gentle. Annie felt certain the color of her cheeks and neck bore a close resemblance to the deep crimson cocktail dress she wore.

"Good evening," she returned with what she hoped was poise. His fingers slid slowly down her arm and came to rest on her hand, which he promptly brought to his lips. The kiss was brief and innocent, but Annie was so taken off guard that she couldn't think clearly. She could only stare.

His black hair waved stylishly to just above his collar. His eyes were silvery gray, compelling, magnetic. When their gazes locked, Annie felt a sizzle zap through her. The sensation reminded her of the jolt she'd gotten when she plugged in the six-slice toaster with the frayed cord.

"Are you traveling alone?" he asked genially.

She nodded, caution preventing her from revealing any details.

"You shouldn't have any difficulty finding a seat then," he said.

Again, Annie nodded, still staring at him. She liked the sound of his voice as much as she liked watching his mouth form the words. His accent was impossible to pin down, and it wasn't one she heard often in the diner. She waited in anticipation for him to say something else.

He lifted an expressive brow. "Is something the matter?"

She swallowed and moistened her lips and swallowed again. "You . . . you look like someone I know."

"Ah," he murmured. He studied her face for a long heartbeat, as if he were absorbed in memorizing every freckle and dimple. Then he smiled. "With such a pretty face, I would remember if we'd met before." With that he raised her fingertips to his lips once more, released her hand, and eased past her. He gave a small salute, then vanished into the mingling crowd.

She stood transfixed for a few seconds, then quickly recovered her mental balance. No doubt soft-toned flattery came easily for a man with such a velvety voice, she decided. Whoever he was, she'd be doing herself a favor to steer clear of him. She checked her watch, noticing that it was nearly show time, and made her way to a plush, cushioned chair in the center of the lounge not far from the stage.

Because she had been one of the last passengers to arrive, she'd scarcely had time to locate her cabin and change clothes before the afternoon show. She had no idea what type of entertainment lay in store for her, but she noticed that the room was almost full.

A six-piece combo was playing a medley of tunes from the big-band era. Annie recognized the hits of Glenn Miller, Tommy Dorsey, and Benny Goodman, thanks to Sadie's selection of jukebox recordings. After a round of applause there was a long drum roll and a middle-aged man dressed in a gleaming white suit swept onto the stage, microphone in hand.

"Ladies and gentlemen, welcome to the Christmas voyage of the Tropicana Cruise Line's newest and most exciting ship in the fleet, the *Tropicana Maxima*. My name is Russell Roth and I'm your cruise director." He took a deep bow, revealing a sizable bald spot on the crown of his head. "This afternoon, for your *Maxima* pleasure, we are indeed fortunate to have on board an internationally renowned entertainer extraordinaire who will soon begin an extended European tour. Please join me in welcoming the recording sensation, Mr. Phillipe Nadeau."

Annie barely heard the thunderous roar of applause

that echoed through the room. The tempo of her heart-beat escalated and she felt her breath catch in her throat when he took his place on center stage.

Phillipe Nadeau. She'd made a first-class fool out of herself in front of Phillipe Nadeau. Of course he looked like someone she knew! Sitting very still, she stared at him. She felt the blood drain from her head and her temples pulsed. Humiliation, so strong that she could taste it, welled up inside her.

How stupidly naive could she be! The ship wasn't five miles from port and already she'd set herself apart from the others. Refined, dignified women didn't ogle like fourteen-year-old schoolgirls. From now on she'd keep her loose lips zipped. Sadie always told her she had a habit of saying the wrong thing at the wrong time.

At least she was honest, she reasoned, which was more than she could say of Phillipe Nadeau. According to the articles she'd read about him, he was quite a ladies' man. He ought to be ashamed of himself. No doubt his flattery worked effectively with the majority of the female population. Annie tried to tell herself that she was the exception.

And then he began to sing. As she listened to the lyrics of the familiar love song, the timbre of his deep voice brought a smile to her lips. He sang another song, then another, each more beautiful than the last. All too soon, he stopped, bowed, and left. Annie glanced at her watch and was surprised to discover an hour had elapsed. She was so absorbed in the music, the mood, and the man, time had stood still.

The combo resumed playing and Annie remained in

her seat. She was suddenly very tired and the soft chair was comfortable. She let her eyes drift closed after a few minutes, feeling warm and relaxed, lulled by the gentle motion of the ship and the strains of the music. The events of the preceding two days reeled through her thoughts in slow motion. The airplane trip . . . the shopping . . . the limousines. . . .

"Excuse me, but are you feeling all right?"

Startled, Annie turned in the direction of the faintly accented voice. She blinked, adjusting her eyes to the now well-lit room, and discovered Phillipe Nadeau was standing behind her. He had changed into a less formal suit, still black, but with a bright red tie.

"Many people suffer from motion sickness their first night out," he continued.

She sat up straighter and looked around the deserted room. "I feel fine," she said, rising abruptly and smoothing her skirt. "If you could tell me how to get to the dining room, I'd be grateful. I'm scheduled for the early sitting."

He flicked up his cuff, revealing a trim gold watch. "I hate to be the bearer of bad news, but your dining companions are probably finishing their dessert by now. I'm going to dinner myself. Would you like to join me?"

Annie sidestepped around her chair. "Join you?" Her mind spun. "Oh, no. I couldn't impose. I'll eat something later at the midnight buffet."

"It's no imposition, I assure you." He smiled and stepped closer.

His smile was tantalizing and seductive, and Annie had the feeling that he knew how to use it to his best advantage. Men like him were dangerous and best avoided, she reminded herself sternly.

"I—I—" Struggling for words, she frantically tried to come up with an excuse. How could she simply refuse without seeming ungracious?

"Come with me," he said with a sweeping motion of his arm. When he offered her his elbow, she took it. Her fingers luxuriated in the smoothness of his sleeve. She caught the subtle scent of his musky cologne. Every instinct she possessed told her she was way out of her league, yet in spite of the alarm bells ringing in her head, she found herself walking down a sweeping flight of stairs. Several people called out greetings to Phillipe. He nodded his head in acknowledgment and hurried along without pausing.

He opened a door and ushered her into the elegant restaurant, which had a decor of plush burgundy and gold. A huge Christmas tree shaped from tier upon tier of live poinsettias stood beneath a sparkling crystal chandelier.

The maître d' led the way to a secluded corner. The private table was flanked by a pair of huge aquariums and the ocean on another side. He pulled out a chair for Annie, and after she was seated, handed her a leather-bound menu.

When the maître d' walked away, Annie turned to the window. "Isn't it beautiful?" she said, sighing, her eyes scanning the darkness. "Have you ever seen more stars? I wonder if it's always like this."

Phillipe shrugged. "I suppose it's pretty much the same every night." He glanced at the menu. "What do you feel like eating?"

Her gaze traveled down the page. "I don't know," she said, struggling with the unfamiliar selections. "What sounds good to you?" As the words tumbled automatically from her lips, she wondered how many times she'd heard a customer ask the same question. How far away the diner seemed now. How very different she felt.

Never lifting his gaze from the menu, he said, "The chateaubriand is a favorite of mine. How about you?"

Annie took a long sip of ice water, wondering how she should respond. There was also the problem of silverware. She had absolutely no idea of the correct sequence in using one, two, three . . . ten! Good grief, there were ten pieces. She glanced at Phillipe and was relieved that his attention was still focused on the menu. Suddenly, he looked up and caught her staring at him.

"Is something wrong?"

"Oh, no. I was just thinking."

Phillipe nodded and smiled. So did Annie. She felt as out of place and conspicuous as a cat at a dog show. Taking a deep, steadying breath, she said, "There are so many choices. I want to read every word before I make up my mind."

Phillipe cocked his head toward her curiously. "Is this your first cruise?"

Was she that obvious? Expressionless, Annie nodded. She started to shake and willed herself to stay under control. *Keep cool,* she instructed herself. The entire scenario was too unbelievable. Annie fought the impulse to pinch herself to see if she was awake. To be sharing a table on a cruise ship with a world-famous celebrity was about as improbable as joining the President for lunch at the White House.

"Would you care for an aperitif, miss?" the waiter asked. *I might if I knew what it was,* she thought to herself. "No, thank you," she told him and turned to look out the window. She heard Phillipe ordering something in French. The lilt of his voice sent her pulse soaring.

The plain truth was, she realized, the idea of cruising around the Caribbean didn't rattle her as much as the man seated across from her. She took another sip of water and looked at him over the rim. His eyes twinkled.

When the wine steward brought a bottle of burgundy, Annie took a few moments to compose herself.

"Would you care for wine?" the man asked.

She nodded, which probably wasn't necessary since he was already filling her wineglass. Seconds later a waiter appeared with a platter of shrimp wrapped in bacon, artfully arranged upon a bed of lettuce.

She watched as Phillipe picked up a small fork and stabbed a piece of shrimp. She did the same. It smelled delicious. She noticed the crusty blackened texture and decided it must have been grilled. She took a bite, chewed, and swallowed. Tears suddenly pooled in her eyes and her throat clogged shut. She grabbed her wine and drank nearly all of it.

"Are you all right?" Phillipe placed his napkin on the table and rose.

"I'm fine," Annie said, gasping. "The shrimp was spicier than I expected."

"It's Cajun," he said, as if that explained everything. "I'll order something milder."

"Oh, no, this is fine." She dabbed the corners of her eyes with her napkin.

He sat down. "More wine?"

Holding her breath, Annie realized she must have given him the impression of being a real lush! Truthfully, she wasn't much of a drinker and had no intention of letting alcohol dull her senses, especially tonight. She cleared her throat. "Could I have some hot tea instead?"

Phillipe merely nodded.

Her cheeks felt as if they were on fire. What must he think of her now? She should be polite, but reserved, Annie decided firmly. She'd order something American-sounding, eat quickly, decline dessert, and excuse herself as soon as she possibly could.

"Have you studied astronomy?" he asked politely.

"What?"

"Astronomy. You seem so preoccupied with the stars, I thought you might have an interest in astronomy."

She turned toward the window. "I can pick out a few constellations." She sighed. "There are so many stars out there tonight, I wouldn't even begin to know where to look for the Big Dipper."

"It occurs to me that I don't even know your name," Phillipe said.

Her name?

Annie turned to face him. His brows were raised expectantly. How should she answer? Did she dare go ahead with her plan? It seemed so feasible when the idea had first come to her. Should she reveal that she'd won the trip and play it safe, or let everyone think she could afford to buy a ticket and thus live out her greatest fantasy? For this one week of her life, should she stick with Annie or step into Anna's shoes? She scooted to the edge of her chair, her eyes wide and clearly focused on her dining companion. It was now or never. The decision was strictly hers.

She slowly extended her right hand across the table, smiled warmly, and said with dignity, "My name is Anna Stewart."

"Anna," he repeated slowly.

Her name floated from his lips like the lyric of a love song. He'd pronounced the word with a soft, European flavor—*Ah-nah*. Her name had never sounded more beautiful to her ears. For an instant, she even felt beautiful.

"Where are you from, Anna?" he prompted.

"Iowa," she returned with a shaky voice, then smiled at the busboy, who set a fresh glass of water in front of her. "Thanks." She took several gulps in an effort to soothe her dry, scratchy throat.

He lifted an expressive brow. "Iowa?"

"It's in the Midwest."

Phillipe nodded several times. "Do you come from a large family?"

Annie shook her head. It was an innocent enough question. She wondered why she felt as if his eyes were boring into her soul. She stiffened and her freshly polished crimson nails dug into the thick, white-linen napkin on her lap. "There's just my brother, Rick, and me."

His features took on an appraising look. "And your parents?"

She drew in a shaky breath and let it out slowly. "Both dead."

He studied her face for a moment or two, then said, "I see." He selected a croissant from the assortment of breads that had been placed on their table, broke it in half, and buttered it.

Annie looked at him speculatively. *What* did he see? How had the conversation taken this turn? The last thing she wanted was to discuss her personal life with Phillipe Nadeau! Somehow she had to steer the topic away from herself.

She managed to chatter about the food, the service, and the surroundings for a while. But by the time they had worked their way through the soup, salad, and main course, Annie found that he was querying her again. She decided she'd better stick as close to the truth as possible.

"You've never married?" Phillipe asked, reaching for the steaming cup of coffee that had been set before him.

"No," Annie replied simply.

"Certainly you're not lacking for male companionship?" he asked, refusing to let the matter rest.

His persistence annoyed her. "I date, if that's what you mean," she said, privately trying to recall the last time she'd gone out with a man. Since her mother's death, she had struggled so hard trying to make a living for herself and Rick, there had been nothing left, no emotion to give to a man.

"Then there's no one special in your life?"

She shook her head. "My life is really pretty boring—probably just the opposite of yours." After a slight pause, she said, "I read somewhere that you own a castle in the south of France."

Phillipe nodded cautiously. "I do."

"Do you spend much time there?"

"Not nearly enough." He leaned his forearms on the table and steepled his hands. "It sits on a deserted peninsula in the middle of nowhere. It's difficult for me to remain there for any length of time."

Annie sipped her hot tea, then asked, "Doesn't it require a lot of care?"

"A small staff lives there. They let me know what needs to be done, and I send them the money."

Cut, dried, organized, impersonal. Annie wondered if he handled the rest of his affairs in equal fashion.

"Do you have a girlfriend?" She regretted the words as soon as they were out of her mouth. What had possessed her to ask such a thing?

Phillipe shook his head. "No." The angular planes of his face shifted into a slight smile.

Annie smiled nervously. "Please forgive me. I have no business prying into your personal affairs." *Affairs*. Goodness, she hadn't actually said that word, had she? She sighed. So much for tact and discretion.

"Please don't feel obligated to make conversation with me, Anna. I much prefer comfortable silence."

Annie's mind whirled at his dry response. She stared in bewilderment at the man seated across the table. Was he trying to tell her that he could do without her company? Or that he was a loner? She suddenly realized that she knew very little about him personally, only what the gossip columnists had written. For all she knew, he could be married with several children. Or be like her father.

Annie shuddered at the thought. Like Phillipe Nadeau, her father was a wealthy, strikingly handsome man. He was also a deceitful, lecherous betrayer, who, although married, had seduced his young housekeeper. When she told him she was pregnant, he refused to acknowledge the child was his. That child was Annie. She had no place in her life for a carousing Casanova.

Struck by the similarities between Phillipe and her father, Annie got to her feet, deciding it was better to leave. ''Thank you for a wonderful dinner, Mr. Nadeau. It was very kind of you to invite me to join you.''

''You're not leaving, are you?'' Phillipe rose, reached out, and caught her wrist, stopping her. ''Don't go,'' he said very quietly. ''I'm sorry if I offended you. I sometimes say things that I later regret.''

Annie studied him for a long moment. ''I don't think I trust you, Mr. Nadeau.''

A corner of his mouth lifted, then he rewarded her with an amused smile. ''You're a wise woman, Anna Stewart.''

A shiver raced down her spine. She didn't feel wise; she felt foolish.

''Let's go out on deck and look at those stars of yours.''

Annie's eyes widened. She looked at him as he stood in front of her, and she thought she never had seen anyone so handsome. She wondered if she was capable of denying any request he might make. But logic intervened. ''I don't think so.''

He looked into her eyes. "All right, then. Have brunch with me tomorrow."

She met his gaze with a direct one of her own. "I'm afraid that's not possible," she managed.

"A late lunch then?"

She shook her head. "I'm scheduled to take the early-morning tour of St. Thomas, and I've arranged to have coffee and fruit sent to my room." Actually, her itinerary was planned in advance by the cruise director, but Phillipe didn't need to know all the details.

"What time is your tour?"

"We leave at eight."

Phillipe swallowed audibly. "In the morning?"

Annie smiled sweetly. "Yes."

He cleared his throat. "It's been quite awhile since I've been to St. Thomas. May I join you?"

She studied him more intently. "Why?"

"Because I have nothing else planned and I want to, that's why."

"Do you always do everything you want?"

"I wouldn't go so far as to say *always,* but usually I do." He smiled, then said, "I'll walk you to your cabin."

"Oh, no," she objected swiftly. "I can find it by myself."

"Listen, I wouldn't dream of abandoning you in a restaurant." He watched her closely. "Do you have a problem with that?"

She had an enormous problem with that, but she wasn't about to tell him. Rather than make a scene in front of the ever-present but silent waiter and busboy, Annie decided to give in. They left the room. He didn't utter a word as they rode the elevator up three floors or walked down the narrow corridor.

When they reached her door, she took a deep, steadying breath and said with what she hoped was firmness, "Good night, Mr. Nadeau." She avoided looking into his eyes and fumbled with her passcard in the narrow slot.

He slid it from her fingers. "Allow me." He inserted it and the lock released with a click. Phillipe opened the door and stepped aside. "Good night, Anna."

"Good night," she managed in a whisper.

"See you tomorrow," he replied and closed the door behind him.

Chapter Three

December twenty-first dawned precisely at six thirty-one. Annie knew because it was the first full day of her vacation, and she was awake in time to watch the sun slip over the horizon. Fortunately, she didn't require a lot of sleep.

Long after Phillipe had left, she lay on the bed and stared out the window into the inky blackness. She recounted each moment of the evening, trying to determine how she had lost control. Why had she agreed to spend the morning with Phillipe Nadeau? But there were no logical answers. Nothing in her life had prepared her for a man like him.

By the time she'd finished her breakfast of hot tea, a toasted bagel, and fresh strawberries, her stomach was tied in knots.

She jumped at the light tap on her door. It was him. She was certain of it. Today she would keep a tight reign on her heartstrings. She was sure of that too. However, the moment she stood face-to-face with Phillipe, all her intentions tottered—along with her composure.

She had no earthly explanation why her mouth sud-

30

denly became powder dry or why her palms grew moist. He was just a man, she reminded herself, taking in his crisply pressed navy trousers and bright red-and-navy striped shirt.

A beguiling smile, much like the one he'd worn the first time she'd seen him, was on his face. "Good morning." He stepped into her cabin. "Are you ready?"

Annie averted her gaze and tried to control the trembling she felt within. "I just need to get my purse." Why, oh, why had she decided to wear the white gauze off-the-shoulder sundress? she thought, self-consciously watching unsightly red blotches surface on her exposed skin. She crossed the floor, and with a tug, hoisted the straps of her canvas bag.

"Allow me."

Annie quivered at the sound of Phillipe's voice so near behind her. She took a deep breath and tried to relax.

He flipped off the lights as they left her cabin, then fell into step beside her in the deserted hallway. "Tell me," he began, "is there a special reason why you booked the earliest tour?"

She grinned shyly. "I didn't want to waste a single minute. Besides, morning is the best time of day."

Phillipe gave a brief nod. "I had a feeling you were a morning person."

Annie wondered to herself, what possible difference could it make to him? She cast him a sidelong glance. He must have been thinking about her. Although it was only an insignificant observation, she was immensely pleased.

The minute she stepped off the ship, Annie stopped to stare. She had ventured into another world. Everything looked and smelled and felt so tropical. She watched a flock of graceful white gulls swoop down to almost touch the water, then soar off with a cry as if they were singing in rhythm with the beat of the surf. The air felt balmy and smelled like ripe citrus.

"Where do we board the tour bus?" Phillipe asked a crew member.

"At the other end of the pier," the uniformed man replied. "It should be a quiet ride. Most people go on the eleven o'clock tour."

"Then they'd miss the afternoon snorkeling lessons," Annie said, turning to Phillipe. "I'm so glad we got an early start. It's such a glorious day."

He pulled a pair of sunglasses from his shirt pocket and slid them on. "And I can't think of a better way to spend it than with you."

Annie could feel her resistance to his charm melting in the warmth of his smile.

"When we get to town," he said, clasping her hand and linking his fingers with hers, "will you go shopping for souvenirs?"

"Souvenirs?" she repeated and wondered what he would think if he knew she had less than thirty dollars in her purse. "No, I thought I'd visit some of the stores and browse." And redeem the certificate for the extravagantly expensive perfume she'd won, she added silently.

They boarded the air-conditioned sight-seeing bus and Annie chose a seat by the window. The crewman's prediction was right: Only a handful of seats were occupied. As the bus pulled away from the pier, the driver's voice came over a loudspeaker.

"Welcome to St. Thomas. Our island is part of the United States Virgin Islands and is often called the American Caribbean Playground. In a few minutes we'll be passing by Magen's Bay. The wide, white beach there has been rated as one of the top ten most beautiful in the world."

With her nose nearly pressed against the window, Annie looked out with wide-eyed delight. The view was a kaleidoscope of colors. From the vivid emerald-green mountains that rose majestically in the background to the vibrant orange, yellow, and red flowers growing along the road, she couldn't imagine a more spectacular place.

"Just look at those little white-and-pink houses built into the hillside!" she exclaimed.

"St. Thomas was settled by the Danish in 1672," the guide continued. "In the days of piracy, the island was a favorite hideout for Captain Kidd and Blackbeard."

"I wish I had a camera," Annie remarked.

Phillipe tapped her shoulder. "Look over there." He pointed to a trio of hang gliders.

Annie turned her head and watched in amazement. She found it difficult to believe that three people were actually attached to the wings of soaring kites and suspended over the ocean. "That looks dangerous," she said. "Have you ever tried it?" She twisted in her seat and suddenly found herself nose to nose with Phillipe. For a few seconds they sat staring at each other.

Then he reached up, his fingers touching the fine wispy hair that had found its way out of the ribbon.

"No, Anna. That's one experience I haven't had."

Phillipe continued to stare into her face. The muscles around her heart constricted. For an instant Annie wondered if she'd ever breathe again. She forced a breath into her lungs, and she gulped. She swallowed convulsively and coughed.

"Are you all right?"

Annie coughed again and nodded. "I'm fine," she said. She felt her cheeks grow pink as she turned her face toward the window.

The bus traveled along a narrow road close to the shore, and she noticed that the ocean was a paler shade of blue, laced with a fringe of white. By contrast, the sand looked like sparkling silver. "I've never seen anything so beautiful in my entire life," she said. "And just think—this afternoon I'll be swimming out there. I wonder if the water's as warm as it looks."

"Did you say something about learning how to snorkel?" Phillipe asked.

She nodded, still facing the window. "My lessons begin at two. I can hardly wait!" She turned toward him. "Do you snorkel?"

He shifted in his seat and shook his head. "I usually don't have much free time."

"Aren't you on vacation?" Annie asked.

"Vacation! Hardly!" He removed his sunglasses and stared directly at her. "What did you think I was doing onstage last night? Relaxing?"

Annie shrank into her seat. "I knew you were performing, but I thought the rest of your time was your own.''

''Unfortunately not. I have people tagging along with me: a production, lighting, and sound crew, backup singers, and a band. If I'm out having a wonderful time, they're out having a wonderful time.''

''You're not working right now,'' she observed aloud.

''That's right. But I'm holding a rehearsal this afternoon.''

''How many people are involved?'' Annie asked.

''I have eighteen men and six women with me this time, just because the stage is small and the acoustics in the lounge are acceptable.''

''So many people away from their families at Christmas,'' Annie said, suddenly melancholy.

''That's business,'' Phillipe returned. ''As they say, the show must go on. And for every show there's a minimum of four hours of practice.''

''Always before the show?'' Annie asked, still trying to digest this new information.

''Always before the show, and,'' he added solemnly, ''every morning for about three hours after the last show.''

''But your last show doesn't end until after midnight, does it?''

He nodded. ''That's right. The best time to practice on a cruise ship is when the passengers are asleep. There are fewer interruptions that way.''

''But that means. . . .'' Annie's voice trailed off in mid-sentence as she noticed for the first time the telltale signs of exhaustion on his face. Crinkly little lines extended from the corners of his eyes, and faint dark circles spread beneath them. "You didn't get much sleep last night, did you?"

"No."

"Then why did you insist on joining me?"

"Because I wanted to, that's why." He put his dark glasses back on. "What else can I say? I've lapsed into temporary insanity. Why do you ask so many questions?"

Annie shrugged and turned back toward the window.

When they reached the main street of St. Thomas and got off the bus, she recognized the name of the shop on her certificate right away. "Let's go into Rio's," she said, wondering how she would go about choosing her gift without revealing the details to her companion.

Before they could step through the arched brick entrance, a young woman touched Phillipe's arm.

As he turned in her direction, she said, "It really *is* you! I can't believe it. I've got all your CDs. My name's Kelly Fisher." She extended a slender, perfectly manicured hand. Phillipe accepted it enthusiastically with a five-hundred-watt smile.

"It's always a pleasure to meet a fan," he said, giving her his full attention. "Where are you from?"

From her deep Southern drawl, Annie guessed Alabama. "Georgia," Kelly said. Her short, pale blond hair was swept away from her face, and Annie suspected she went through a jumbo economy-size bottle of styling mousse every week to keep her gravity-defying bangs from flopping into her face. The style,

Annie noted, was quite a contrast to her own modestly ribboned ponytail.

"Your *Moonlight and Memories* CD is my absolute favorite," the girl cooed. "I play it every morning on my way to Georgia State."

"So you're a college student," Phillipe replied, continuing to smile.

Annie rocked back on her heels while Kelly recounted her subjects, described her roommates, and went into detail about her future plans as a marine biologist. Annie tuned out the conversation and tuned in the flirtatious expressions both Phillipe and Kelly were exchanging. And why not? she asked herself. The young beauty was certainly his type. Intelligent, articulate, attractive—traits that were more than emphasized by the iridescent blue T-shirt and neon-pink shorts that hugged her lean body like a second skin.

"I'm going to go ahead into the store," Annie said, interrupting the flow of their conversation. Phillipe nodded and smiled.

Ten minutes later she left the boutique and found Phillipe in front of the camera store next door, talking with a middle-aged couple and their two teenage daughters. What had happened to Kelly? Annie wondered, watching Phillipe wave at her.

While his attention was focused on signing autographs and talking with his fans, Annie took the opportunity to study him in greater detail. She noticed for the first time a faint scar above his left eyebrow. His teeth, even and white, contrasted pleasantly with his olive skin. Without a doubt, Phillipe Nadeau was one of the most physically appealing men she had ever met. Annie found herself wishing that their worlds weren't so far apart.

Every now and then she had moments when she felt a pang of loneliness. This was one of those times. It was contrary to her nature to give in to self-pity, but she wouldn't be human if she didn't regret that there was no one special in her life. She wondered if the right man would ever come along. In fact, she wasn't sure such a man existed. Deep down inside, Annie knew that just anyone wouldn't do. She wanted to experience that all-consuming love that every woman hopes will be hers. But how should she go about finding it?

Before she could tuck her stray thoughts back into her head, a short, plump, gray-haired woman wearing a loose-fitting tropical-print shift burst into the group of fans. She immediately began to pump Phillipe's hand.

"Phillipe Nadeau! Right here on the street! Imagine! My husband and I caught your show in Vegas last summer." Phillipe smiled politely and tried to extract his hand. Without a pause nor relinquishing her hold, the woman continued. "I don't suppose you have any autographed pictures with you?"

Phillipe stepped closer to Annie. The woman moved with him. "I'm afraid not. I believe the cruise director on the *Maxima* has plenty, though."

"The *Maxima,*" the woman said with a sigh. "That's the ship I told Howard to book us on. We're stuck on the *Gateway to Paradise*. Wouldn't you know!"

"Ah, yes," Phillipe mumbled, finally freeing his

hand. "It was a pleasure meeting all of you. Now, if you'll excuse me, this patient woman beside me is expecting me to join her for lunch." He swiftly removed the shopping bag from Annie with one hand, and linked his other with her fingers.

"I thought that poor woman was going to shake off your arm. She was so excited, I wouldn't be surprised if she tried to transfer her ticket to our ship," Annie said.

Phillipe nodded. "She did get a bit carried away. I wish I could say people were more—"

"Mr. Nadeau? Phillipe Nadeau?" A stylish older woman with a puff of light-pink cotton-candy hair nudged her way next to him on the narrow cobblestone sidewalk. "I'm Louise Gerhardt and I just think you're the ultimate! How about a little kiss, right here?" She pointed to a spot on her more than adequately rouged cheek.

Instead, Phillipe gently grasped her diamond-clad hand and briefly brought it to his lips. "I'm delighted to meet you, Mrs. Gerhardt."

"Oh, the pleasure is mine," the woman replied, then without stopping to draw a breath, she continued. "You're a lot taller in person than I thought you'd be. What are you, about six foot three?"

Phillipe took a step backward. "Six-two."

The woman stepped forward, slid her arm through Phillipe's, and gave a squeeze. "And muscular too. You know, I have a granddaughter who's about your age. She's an accountant and recently divorced. Lovely girl. Top in her class at—"

Annie took one look at the pained expression of

tolerance on Phillipe's face and piped up. "Excuse me, Mrs. Gerhardt," she cut in, "would you happen to be from eastern Pennsylvania?"

"Why, yes," the woman returned hesitantly, releasing her grasp from Phillipe. "I'm from Philadelphia. How did you know?"

Annie smiled sweetly. "My Aunt Sylvia is from there and she's always trying to marry off one of my cousins. You remind me so much of her."

The woman stood dumbfounded for a few seconds, then cleared her throat. "I didn't realize this woman was with you, Mr. Nadeau."

Phillipe laid his hand on Annie's shoulder. "Indeed she is."

"Well, I'll say good-bye then," Mrs. Gerhardt muttered, stepping off the curb.

Annie drew a deep breath and let it out on a sigh. She looked up at Phillipe, to find him staring at the woman's retreating back. Her first thought was that she'd offended him by taking matters into her own hands.

"Sorry if I made a mistake by—"

"No, no, you handled the situation perfectly. This is one of the few times I didn't have to think of a subtle way to send a fan on her way." He shook his head. "How did you know where she was from?"

"Her granddaughter."

"Pardon me?"

"It was the way she said the word 'granddaughter,' " Annie explained. "Did you notice how she said 'granddaughter' using the letter d instead of t?"

Phillipe's eyebrows rose expressively, as if the revelation explained nothing. "There must be more to it than that," he said as they resumed walking.

She hesitated, not sure how much she wanted him to know about her fascination with dialects. If he wondered how she had perfected her talent, then what would she say? Certainly not that after working along an interstate highway for seven years and listening to truckers from all over the country she'd learned how to distinguish speech patterns and determine a person's origins. She swallowed and said simply, "Linguistics is my hobby."

To Annie's relief, the loud, piercing noise from a street crew repairing the pavement at an intersection precluded conversation for a few seconds. When the hammering ceased, Phillipe asked, "Would you mind having lunch on the ship? I'd like to get away from the crowds and noise for a while."

Annie tilted her head at Phillipe and smiled. "Wonderful food, glorious surroundings, a fabulous view? It's probably the best place to eat on the island," she mused.

His arm slid around her waist. "Thank you," he whispered and promptly hailed a cab.

A half-hour later, seated at the practically deserted poolside pub on the Veranda deck, Phillipe said, "I'm sorry you didn't have a chance to do more shopping."

Annie shifted in her chair. "Shopping has never been on my list of favorite things to do."

The waiter sat a tall glass of iced tea in front of her. "Are you ready to order?"

She glanced at Phillipe, who in turn gestured for her to go ahead. Without giving regard to the menu selections, she said, "I'd like a small tossed salad with ranch dressing and a cheeseburger, medium-well, with lettuce, tomato, mustard, and pickles, please."

The waiter's mouth twitched beneath his pencil-thin mustache as he made note of her preferences. "And for you, sir?"

"I'll have the broccoli cheese soup, a spinach salad, and coffee," Phillipe said, his eyes never straying from Annie's. The moment they were alone, he leaned back in his chair and crossed his arms over his chest.

"Is something wrong?" she asked.

"No, but I'm curious about something."

"About me?"

He smiled and inclined his head. "What *is* on your list of favorite things to do?"

She took a slow sip of tea and looked at the sparkling blue waters of the Caribbean below her. No one had ever asked her that before. For as long as she could remember she'd kept a mental list of fun and exciting things she dreamed of doing someday. "Flying in an airplane high above fat, puffy white clouds, and sinking up to my chin in an enormous bathtub filled with lilac-scented bubbles," she said wistfully, immensely pleased that in the past few days she'd done exactly that.

"Not both at the same time, I hope," Phillipe teased.

Seeing the amusement in his eyes, she laughed, then smiled at the waiter as he served her salad.

"It's so fascinating to sit here and watch the people and the water and the sky . . . and everything." She laughed again. "I never dreamed it would be like this! Even the weather is perfect. I still can't believe I got on the plane in the middle of a snowstorm and got off to swaying palm trees and sunshine!''

Then she met his glance. There was something judgmental in his look that instantaneously altered her mood. The glare of the sun reflecting off the pool water bathed him in an aura of gold, reminding her that he was a celebrity, a star. And here she was babbling about the scenery!

''You're an interesting woman, Anna Stewart,'' Phillipe said, nodding slightly.

Annie found herself at a loss for words. Phillipe Nadeau thought *she* was interesting? That was a masterpiece of misinterpretation. If only he knew the truth.

''Do you enjoy being an entertainer?'' she asked, regarding him with somber curiosity.

He looked as if he were weighing the question, then said, ''For the most part, yes. However, people in the entertainment industry have no life of their own.'' He added cream to his coffee and stirred slowly. ''When I'm not onstage, I'm hounded by reporters who exaggerate every trivial detail of my life, or I'm chased by women young enough to be my daughters or old enough to be my grandmother, such as Mrs. Gerhardt. Singing, I enjoy. Putting up with thoughtless, tactless, insensitive women, I find difficult to tolerate.'' His voice trailed away. He'd said enough.

A sudden chill hung on the edge of his words. Annie pushed aside the remainder of her salad, her appetite suddenly gone. His statement had angered her, and she flashed him a look of disdain. ''So you don't like women?''

''I beg your pardon,'' he replied, puzzled. ''I most

certainly do! Why on earth would you say such a thing?''

She lifted her chin, meeting his gaze straight on. ''I'm finding it difficult to believe that you find women so . . . so. . . .''

The waiter silently slid their food onto the table and left.

''Go on,'' Phillipe said, stabbing a spinach leaf.

''Distasteful.'' Uneasiness spiraled down her spine, making her sit up straight on the edge of her chair. She had been right. Phillipe Nadeau was nothing more than a playboy. In public, his displays of affection seemed genuine, but in private, now Annie knew better. And what about her? she wondered. Did he consider her a bothersome fan? Was he using her for his own selfish pleasure? ''What kind of a man are you?'' she said in a rush of emotion.

His eyes sparked with irritation. ''A human one.'' Phillipe raked his hand through his hair. ''For the life of me, I don't know why we're having this ridiculous conversation. You enjoy baiting me, don't you?''

''No,'' Annie said firmly. She took a bite of her cheeseburger and dabbed a drip of mustard from the side of her mouth with her napkin. She narrowed her eyes accusingly. ''You put on quite a performance.'' Just like her father.

Phillipe threw up his arms in exasperation. ''I'm a performer! I get paid to entertain.''

''But the affection you give to women is just part of your act,'' she accused.

''Not every single aspect of it, no. I enjoy being with an attractive woman as much as any man, but most of them have no interest in me personally. And when I'm entertaining, I try to give my audiences what they pay for.''

''So you sacrifice yourself to please the public?''

''I entertain,'' he repeated simply while tightening his fingers around the delicate stem of a water goblet.

''Only *some* women repulse you, then?'' she added dryly.

He shrugged, not bothering to deny it. ''In the past twelve years, women have pulled every trick in the book to get their hooks into me.''

''You must consider yourself quite a catch.''

''I'm a realist, or I try to be. I've put up with bored housewives, lusty college girls, and wealthy matrons. They've taught me things about trickery, perjury, entrapment, dishonesty. . . .'' He ticked off the evils on his fingers.

Annie bristled. ''It's a wonder men still allow women to mingle in society—we're such malicious and dangerous creatures.''

''Not all women are offensive. Just a few select types.''

''I'm curious,'' Annie said, taking another bite of her burger. ''How many types are there?''

''Dozens.''

''I never knew there were so many.''

''You probably never took time to analyze the subject.''

''And you obviously have.''

He chose not to comment, but glared at her mutely.

Annie suddenly grew quiet, staring at the banner of flags flapping in the breeze above the pool. When she spoke, her voice was serious and low. "Why did you invite me to lunch?"

"Pardon?" he asked, arching a brow. He met her stare evenly.

"I just wondered if inviting me was something you felt obligated to do," she said.

"I hate eating alone."

Annie rolled her eyes skyward. "There must be a hundred women on this ship who'd stand in line all morning to eat lunch with you," she replied, leveling her gaze. "Do you mind telling me why you picked me?"

"Actually, I was drawn to you out of curiosity," he said, his expression bland and unreadable. He popped a crouton into his mouth.

"What makes you curious?" she pressed on.

Shrugging, he said, "You're an enigma."

Her stomach lurched. But her face was all innocence as she looked up at him. "You mean I don't fit into one of your carefully researched categories?" she asked.

There was a pause, as if he were carefully contemplating his response. "No, you don't," he replied finally, leaning back in his chair.

Annie studied him briefly, then said, "I can assure you that there are plenty of women who don't fit neatly into molds." She lifted her chin a fraction.

"Not in my experience." He paused, looking across at her with narrowed eyes, so that any expression was hidden.

"How fortunate you're such an expert on judging

women. No doubt you've sampled quite a few." She regarded him challengingly.

There was a nearly imperceptible tightening of his lips. "I've known my share of women." His tone said clearly that he didn't want to discuss the matter.

Annie ignored the unspoken message. "Well, you're looking at one woman who isn't willing to be sampled."

"Is that so?" Phillipe shot back. He gave her a long, penetrating look.

She met his look unblinkingly.

A muscle in his face twitched. He was a man who liked to dominate others, Annie thought. He'd admitted last night that he almost always got what he wanted. Bidding him a fond farewell would be the sensible thing to do. She had absolutely no business granting Phillipe Nadeau even the slightest entrance into her life. But it was too late, she realized. She already had.

Despite her misgivings, she was intrigued by him. She wanted to get to know him better, but on her own terms. She was sorely tempted to tell him she was a truck-stop waitress without a penny to spare, but she knew that he would immediately cast her aside. She hesitated to guess which of his categories applied to waitresses. The very idea made her shudder. It was pathetic that a man who had the potential for living life to the fullest was so cynical and calculating.

In her opinion, Mr. High-and-Mighty had a few lessons to learn. The top one on the list was to respect people for themselves, and not to judge them on their social class or background. And who better to teach him than herself? she thought. But how could she handle him most effectively? A sudden inspiration struck her.

"It might be best," she said, swirling a straw through the melting ice cubes in her glass, "if we didn't spend any more time together."

"Why?" he asked quickly. "We obviously have our differences in opinion, but what harm could it do if we got to know each other better?"

He'd nibbled at the bait, Annie mused with delight. Her voice remained doubtful and she said, "I don't think that's a good idea."

"Why? Do you have something to hide?"

"No," she replied calmly. "I just think we have very little in common."

"We may be more suited than you realize."

"I sincerely doubt it."

"I don't."

Annie smiled a secret smile. He'd sprung the trap. Before she could fortify her strategy further, a lanky young man with longer-than-average brown hair and an earring in his right ear dashed over to their table.

"Boss! Where have you been? Morris, Dell, and I have been looking all over for you!"

Phillipe scooted back his chair. "What's the problem, Randy?"

"The problem is that Nadine, your new backup singer, is so seasick she can't even sit up."

"The boat isn't even moving, for Pete's sake," Phillipe admonished.

"Well, it was last night. Besides, I think she's pregnant."

"Pregnant!" Phillipe's voice carried enough on the

breeze to cause several passengers to stare openly. "She didn't mention anything about being pregnant when I hired her last week," he all but whispered.

Randy shrugged. "She's pretty sick."

Phillipe stood. "I'll take her to the infirmary and see if they can give her something."

"Some warm mint tea and fresh air would do her a world of good," Annie said quietly.

Both men turned to face her. "Who's she?" Randy asked.

"I'm sorry I didn't introduce you," Phillipe replied. "This is Randy McKinney, my drummer and leader of the band. Randy, this is Anna Stewart."

"It's a pleasure meeting you, Randy," Annie said, offering her hand. "Aren't you originally from the Boston area?"

"Yeah, I grew up in Quincy," the drummer replied. "How did you know that?"

"Just a lucky guess," she said with a smile of satisfaction. New England dialects were among the easiest for her to detect. Hundreds of truckers from the East stopped at Sadie's every day.

For a moment Phillipe studied her intently. *Good,* Annie thought to herself. She meant to keep him guessing. That was part of her plan. She grinned mischievously.

Finally he turned to Randy. "Please tell Nadine I'll order some warm tea and have it sent to her room. After she drinks it, escort her to the uppermost deck and find her a comfortable chair. I'll meet you up there."

"I'm on my way," Randy called over his shoulder.

Phillipe inhaled a deep breath and let it out slowly. He faced Annie, his hands firmly planted on his hips. "When can I see you again?"

She managed to shrug and say offhandedly, "We're shipmates. I'm sure we'll run into each other from time to time."

"You can count on it," Phillipe replied. He touched his forehead slightly in a salute and was gone.

Chapter Four

Phillipe stopped to sign an autograph for an elderly couple on the way back to his suite, but his attention was directed elsewhere. Anna Stewart could become addictive, he realized after he mistakenly wrote *All my love to Anna* instead of *Alma* as the woman had requested. The realization of the extent that Anna had invaded his thoughts disturbed him. As tempting as she was, he reminded himself, she was also trouble.

Women always were.

And the timing couldn't be worse. For the past year and a half his singing career had skyrocketed. His calendar for the following year was already filled. Likewise his business investments had done exceedingly well. Phillipe was realistic enough to know that without devoting time and attention to both, either situation could quickly disappear. He didn't need any distractions.

He sprinted up a flight of stairs and dashed into his suite. After ordering a pot of warm herbal tea for Nadine, he grabbed a stack of sheet music and headed to rehearsal.

"You're ten minutes late," Morris, the bass player, said while tuning his instrument.

"I must be slipping," Phillipe replied dryly. He took a quick head count. Satisfied that all were present or accounted for, he sat down at the piano bench.

Dell, who was pushing seventy but still hit the hauntingly low notes on the saxophone like few in the business, leaned one elbow on the baby grand and smiled. "Old age is catching up with you. Didn't you turn over thirty big ones a couple of weeks ago?"

"That's right," Phillipe said. He looked Dell straight in the eye. "I guess you're going to tell me the memory is always the first to go."

Dell shrugged. "Could be vision." He picked up the score of a new song Phillipe had been working on and held it at arm's length. "Can you read this?"

"With my eyes closed," Phillipe assured him.

"Next thing we know, you'll get married." Dell shook his head. "Midlife crisis, they call it. It's bound to happen sooner or later." He clucked his tongue. "Haven't I been telling you, you're not as fast these days? If you're not careful, one of those women who's always chasing you is going to catch you!"

"Not unless I *want* to be caught," Phillipe quipped, the barest hint of a smile curling his lips.

Dell grinned. "It's just a matter of time." He shuffled off, mumbling something about babies and station wagons.

Phillipe sighed and gazed around him. Most of the band members were either snickering or whispering to one another. He made a gesture of dismissal. "Let's start with the Christmas singalong numbers," he directed. ''I want to be out of here in less than two hours, so let's make this a good one.''

Even minus one singer, rehearsal went smoothly. ''I'll see you at nine-thirty,'' Phillipe called to Dell.

''Not if the blonde finds you first,'' Dell taunted. ''I saw the way you were following her around this morning. Like a pup on a leash. Yes, sir, it's just a matter of time.'' He chuckled on his way out.

Dell couldn't be right, could he? Phillipe thought, disgruntled. He wasn't old enough to be going through a midlife crisis, was he? He rubbed his eyes, trying to ease the dry, burning sensation. ''Old age,'' he grumbled miserably, staring at the sheet of music that blurred before his eyes. He sighed and set it aside. What was it going to be like in another ten years?

Randy walked up and laid his hand on Phillipe's shoulder. ''You look beat. Why don't you try to catch a couple of Zs?''

''That's not a bad idea. Can you handle any catastrophes?''

Randy gave a thumbs-up sign. ''That's what you pay me for.''

Phillipe was detained three times by fans on his way back to his suite. When he finally reached his cabin, he heard a familiar voice call out his name. He turned to find Blake Emerson walking toward him.

''I hope you're still planning to join us for dinner tonight,'' the captain said.

''I wouldn't miss it.''

Blake smiled. ''I can't tell you enough how much I appreciate your being here. I'm sure you'd much rather be home with your family for Christmas.''

Phillipe nodded woodenly.

"You look exhausted. You really should try to get some shut-eye."

After his friend left, Phillipe would have gone straight to sleep. But something Blake had said gave him reason to lie awake. Home. Up until that moment, he hadn't given any thought to spending the holidays with his family. No one had invited him. He guessed his parents were spending Christmas with his Aunt Bernadette in London again. They hadn't included him in their holiday plans for the last decade, so why should they now?

Home. He couldn't get the word out of his mind. Where *was* his home? France, he guessed. He owned some property there. But then he also had a coop in New York City. It had never mattered to him where he lived. Over the years he'd grown used to the convenience of hotels. He gave the suite a disgruntled look. It was nice. Adequately furnished. Comfortable. But *he* wasn't comfortable. He was restless.

He sighed deeply and closed his eyes. A clear picture of Anna Stewart formed in his mind. Her honey-blond hair, styled full and luxurious, made a perfect frame for her heart-shaped face. Although feminine, hers was a strong face, he reflected, the face of a woman accustomed to making her own way in the world. Yet there was also an innocence. He'd noticed that she wore only subtle shades of eye shadow and naturally tinted lipsticks. Too much makeup would have made her look like a child playing a grownup.

He rolled onto his side and scowled. This wasn't the first time Anna had intruded into his thoughts. Snatches of conversations he'd had with her and vivid images of her smile invaded his thoughts when he least expected it. Like now. It distracted and annoyed him. Yet he wanted to see her again.

What did Anna want? What were her future plans? Did she have ambitions, dreams? Probably so. It interested him to know what they were. He drifted off to sleep, wondering how she'd spent her afternoon . . . and with whom she had spent it.

Two long blasts from the ship's whistle announcing the departure from St. Thomas awakened Phillipe. He absently ran his fingers through his hair. A glance at his watch told him he'd slept for nearly two hours. He needed a shower. He needed to order some flowers for Blake's wife and stepdaughter. He needed to check on Nadine. He needed to see Anna.

He found her on the Lido deck near the pool. For a few minutes he merely stood and stared at her. It took a second longer for him to notice the man who was sitting with her. If her stream of chatter was any indication, she'd been talking to him for quite a while. Phillipe watched her tilt back her head and laugh, obviously enjoying herself.

The man was clearly attracted to her, he decided, observing that he had his arm draped along the back of her lounge chair. He looked decent enough, although it was hard to tell from a distance. Phillipe guessed he was about his own age, perhaps a bit younger. He watched as the man's arm slid from the chair to Anna's shoulder. He felt powerfully jealous and that fact stunned him. He had no right to feel such strong emotions. Knowing he could feel so possessive toward her after such a short acquaintance shook him to his soul. A frown settled on his face.

When an obnoxious hulk of a man wearing a pair of neon-orange swim trunks bellowed Anna's name and waved from the diving board, Phillipe could no longer stand idly by. His competitive nature propelled him to join the game. The frown left him, replaced by a determined grin.

"Having a good time?" came a familiar voice from behind Annie.

Startled, she turned to find Phillipe studying her from his position near the railing just a few feet away. His unexpected appearance sent a surge of excitement through her.

"Everything is even better than I imagined," she heard herself say breathlessly. When he smiled, an unwelcome blush crept into Annie's cheeks. Her heart thudded crazily.

As he came toward her, the newly acquainted fellow passenger rose abruptly and hurried off toward the pool. "Do you mind if I join you?" Phillipe asked. Not waiting for a reply, he slipped into the vacant chair.

Annie willed herself to be calm. "How's Nadine?" she asked, trying to act nonchalant.

"Much better." Phillipe smiled and shook his head. "She said to thank you for recommending the tea. So, did you learn all there was to know about snorkeling this afternoon?"

Annie shook her head. "Would you believe the instructor got his foot tangled in a rope and broke his ankle? The purser couldn't find anyone else certified

to teach the group, so he canceled the lesson. I stayed
on the ship and met—''

''A drink for madam.'' Kent Harper, her new acquaintance, returned unexpectedly and offered her a
huge, frothy concoction that looked to Annie like an
iceberg floating in a fishbowl. She accepted the drink
and noticed at the same time that Phillipe had risen.
The two men stood facing each other—one tall, dark,
and worldly; the other short, fair, and innocent-
looking. During the twenty-minute conversation she'd
had with Kent, she had discovered he was not the most
humble of men. Actually, she found him a bit of a
braggart, but he seemed to recognize when he should
exercise humility.

''Phillipe Nadeau, isn't it?'' Kent thrust out his hand
with a quick, awkward movement, and his face lit up
eagerly.

Phillipe nodded and took his sweet time before offering his handshake.

''Nice to meet you!'' Kent returned. ''I've heard a
lot about you.''

Annie knew it had to be her imagination, but in spite
of herself, she could have sworn she saw jealousy in
Phillipe's eyes.

''Perhaps Anna will have a chance to visit with you
later,'' he was saying to Kent, as he smoothly lifted
the glass from her hand and set it on the table. ''If
you'll excuse us, the captain is expecting Anna to join
him in his quarters.''

Stunned, Annie stared up at him.

''Shall we?'' His voice was calm and authoritative.
She braced herself in her chair and eyed him warily.

Without another word, he gently pulled her to her feet. Before he could steer her away, Kent reached out and casually touched her shoulder. ''Perhaps I'll see you later this evening,'' he said wistfully.

Phillipe led Annie away before she could respond. As they moved through the crowd mingling around the pool, her temper seethed. Just who did Mr. Entertainment think he was? And his behavior! It irked her to think of his rudeness to Kent. Phillipe had an abrasive side, and as soon as they had a moment of privacy, she intended to tell him so.

He swept her through a set of doors and into the coolness of the lobby. When the glass doors swished shut behind them, Annie firmly planted her feet onto the plush carpeting. ''Where do you think you're taking me?'' she challenged.

''I told you, we're going to the captain's quarters.'' Phillipe walked over to the elevators and pushed the up button.

''I don't believe you,'' she shot back, her patience at an end.

Phillipe smiled pleasantly. ''Well, you'd better. His stateroom is just above us.''

Annie stared at him suspiciously. ''Why does he want to see *me*?'' she wanted to know.

''Blake Emerson is a good friend of mine. He enjoys meeting his passengers.''

Annie caught a glimpse of her reflection in the chrome elevator doors. Her hair was disheveled from the breeze, her skin was oily from sun lotion, and she was wearing shorts, for heaven's sake. ''I couldn't possibly meet the captain now. I look awful!''

"You look sensational to me," Phillipe replied.

"Oh, no I don't," she snapped, a little off-balance at the way he was looking at her. "I'd like to go to my cabin and make myself presentable."

"Fine. I'll go with you."

Annie placed her hands on her hips. "I'll meet you in the lobby in a half hour.

"Unless you meet someone else first."

"What's that supposed to mean?"

"That teenager by the pool seemed interested enough in you. Maybe you'll decide to meet him instead."

"For your information," Annie blurted, "he isn't a teenager. He programs computers for a company in Los Angeles."

"*Pardonez moi,*" Phillipe returned quickly. "Whether he's a man or a boy, he only had one thing on his mind." His brows drew together in an angry frown. "I don't suppose it occurred to you he expected something in return."

Annie quivered at the insinuation. Did he think she was utterly naive? Of course it had occurred to her! Of all the nerve! The elevator doors opened and she got in. Phillipe followed her and the doors eased closed.

Annie felt the blood rush to her face. How dare this—this Casanova tell *her* how she should conduct herself! "I can assure you that I have no intention of making myself available to every man who wanders my way."

"That's a relief." His hand took possession of her elbow. Immediately she tried to withdraw it, but he held on firmly. "Anna Stewart," he said softly, "I think you've led a sheltered life."

Her face grew scarlet. "I have not! I live with my twenty-year-old half-brother, and I'm hardly a stranger to the methods of the male species."

"I apologize for my hasty conclusions." His expression was one of pained tolerance.

"I accept your apology," Annie said calmly. When the elevator doors opened, she walked out alone without a backward glance. Her knees were shaking.

"Anna."

She flinched at the irritation in his voice. She stopped walking and turned slowly to face him.

"I wasn't finished speaking with you."

"Perhaps I was finished listening."

For a moment he merely stood there, indignant and angry. When he spoke, however, his voice was oddly gentle. "Anna, there are certain . . . how can I put this? . . . cultural differences on this ship you may not have dealt with before. I don't want you trapped in a compromising situation."

Annie kept her eyes focused on the hallway floor. She struggled for the composure to lift her head, and after a moment she found it. "While I appreciate your concern"—it was obvious by her scowl she did not— "I assure you that I can take care of myself." His superiority and smugness infuriated her.

He tilted his head to one side. "Can you really?" By the smirk on his lips, Annie could guess that he doubted she was capable of handling a simple task like feeding herself.

"Believe me, there isn't a line I haven't heard or a

trick that hasn't been tried on me,'' she heard herself say coolly, and felt a brief flare of pride that she had managed to keep things under control. She released an exasperated sigh. ''Why are you so interested in my well-being?''

''Why?'' He lifted his dark brows and studied her. ''Because when I watched you walk onto the ship yesterday afternoon and looked down at the expression of sheer delight on your pretty face, I decided I wanted to get to know you.''

''You were spying on me?''

A smile played about his lips. ''Absolutely!'' He glanced quickly at his watch. ''It's nearly five—I hadn't realized it was so late.'' He pulled her down the corridor at such a fast pace that Annie had to spring to avoid being dragged. ''The captain's cocktail party starts at six,'' he said, then stopped at her door. ''I'll pick you up in fifty-five minutes.''

Annie didn't know how to respond. She'd never met a man so domineering, so sure of himself, so . . . so assuming. Or so appealing. He deftly slid the passcard from her fingers, opened the door, and was on his way before she could utter a word. Baffled, she watched his retreating back as he headed toward the elevators. Then, suddenly, she realized she had less than an hour to make herself presentable. Not just presentable, she corrected herself, stunning, giving herself a little twirl behind the privacy of her closed door.

She stepped out of her clothes and within seconds was reveling in the pulsating spray of steamy water that pelted her skin. It felt luxuriously good. At home in her trailer the water pressure was minimal and the temperature lukewarm at best. She wished she could take a nice, long shower, but there wasn't time.

She toweled off, sprayed herself lightly with the expensive perfume she'd won, and surveyed the contents of her closet. What do people wear to meet the captain? she wondered. After ruling out several options, she slipped on a royal-blue, knee-length cocktail dress. The silky material felt cool against her skin.

She brushed her hair away from her face, securing it with a pair of gold combs, just as the beautician in Miami had shown her, in a sophisticated style that swirled about her shoulders. She slid her feet into shimmering gold heels and leaned closer to the mirror to peer at her reflection. Her eyes were sparkling with excitement and she knew it wasn't because she was meeting the captain. She was spending the next few hours with Phillipe Nadeau and the thought was exhilarating—and scary.

She had just put on a light rose lip gloss when there was a knock at her cabin door.

"Good evening," Phillipe said as she opened the door. "Anna, you look sensational."

"Thank you. So do you." The man *was* exquisite—there was no other word for it. He made her heart jump at the sight of him, as no man had ever done. *What if I fall in love with him?* she thought in sudden panic.

"Are you ready?" he asked.

Annie nodded mutely and wondered if her legs would support her long enough to make it to their destination. She picked up her matching evening bag and fairly floated out the door.

Phillipe's hand rested lightly on the small of her

back as they walked into the captain's gala. She was jittery and excited, and she smiled to herself, amused. No one back home would ever believe that Annie Stewart could be entertained in such style or escorted by such a man.

The reception, however, didn't turn out as Annie had envisioned. After shaking hands with Captain Emerson and having her picture taken by the ship's photographer, she was virtually pushed aside as fans swarmed around Phillipe waving large, glossy, color photos.

"There's plenty for everyone," Russell Roth, the cruise director, said as he cheerfully distributed more pictures. He handed one to Annie. "I'm sure Mr. Nadeau will be happy to sign this for you. Ladies! Please!" he called to three women who were pushing and elbowing their way through the crowd. "Let's form a line."

Phillipe reached for Annie's hand and tugged her to his side. "I'm sorry," he whispered. "It looks like I'm going to be busy for a while."

"I understand."

"I have a commitment for dinner. Perhaps we could meet later—will you be at the show?"

Annie smiled. "I wouldn't miss it."

Phillipe kissed her softly on the temple. "I'll look for you."

"Will you pose with my daughter for a picture, Mr. Nadeau?" an auburn-haired woman asked.

"It would be my pleasure," Phillipe answered, releasing Annie's hand. A freckle-faced girl of about twelve smiled shyly up at him. "What's your name, *ma cherie*?" he asked.

"Stacy," she whispered.

"It's a pleasure to meet you, Stacy." Phillipe took the girl's small hand in his, and kissed it gallantly. A splash of vivid color covered Stacy's cheeks. "Where are you from?" he asked while signing his autograph on a picture.

"Denver," Annie heard the girl say. Her mother waited for Annie to step aside before snapping the picture.

Within seconds she found herself alone in a room full of strangers. She made her way to the door and decided to go up to the dining room. Dinner would be served soon, and she thought she might need some extra time to locate her assigned table.

A few couples were already seated when she arrived. Table thirty-seven was next to a window, and was already occupied by a middle-aged couple who were chatting with each other as Annie approached.

"Excuse me," she said, interrupting their conversation. "I'm your tablemate."

"It's about time you showed up!" the man said, rising and holding out a chair for Annie. His voice was deep and dusty. She already knew he was a Texan. "We thought you'd fallen overboard." He extended a hand. "My name's Forrest Greene, and this sweet young thing is my bride, Ruby."

"Ruby and Forrest Greene?" Annie repeated, certain that the smiling big bear of a man was teasing her.

"That's what it says on our marriage certificate," Ruby said with a laugh. Her blue eyes twinkled as she reached for her spouse's hand. When his palm enclosed hers, Annie marveled at their difference in size. Ruby Greene was as petite as her husband was husky.

"Are you newlyweds?" Annie asked as she scooted up to the table.

"Yup," Forrest replied without hesitation. "And we've been on our honeymoon for the past thirty-two years." He winked at his wife and returned to his seat. "I take it you're traveling solo?"

"That's right. I'm Annie, er, Anna Stewart. This is my first cruise."

"You'll love it, dear," Ruby said, patting Annie's hand. "This is our fifth, and they keep getting better." She chuckled and grinned at her husband.

Annie's heart immediately warmed to the friendly couple. "What part of Texas are you from?" she asked with a mischievous gleam in her eye.

Forrest's bushy gray brows rose. "What makes you think we're Texans?"

"Texans are a special breed of folks," Annie told him. "The twang of your words and the dust on your boots gave you away."

Forrest extended his booted foot out from under the table. "I meant to give these ostrich skins a spit polish before I left the ranch." He took a roll from the bread basket and spread butter on thickly. "I left my Stetson on a hook by the door," he added with a wink.

"Do you own a ranch?" Annie asked.

"Ruby and I are into iron and steel. She irons and I steal," Forrest informed her, all the while keeping a straight face.

"Oh, Forrest!" Ruby admonished. "You ornery

rascal! Don't you ever stop?'' She turned to Annie. ''Forrest and I own a small company that manufactures canvas patio furniture. He used to be a pharmaceutical salesman and he was gone a lot. I stayed home and sewed. About ten years ago we decided to join forces and start a business.''

''It's wonderful you can work together,'' Annie said, thinking how very lucky the Greenes were and what a special relationship they seemed to share. ''Do you have any children?''

''Do we have *children*?'' Forrest pulled his wallet from his pocket.

''Now he'll never stop,'' Ruby said with a laugh. ''We have three sons, a daughter, and nine grandchildren. I hope you like to look at pictures.''

Annie assured them that she did, and for the duration of the meal Forrest and Ruby entertained her with delightful anecdotes of their family.

''Ruby and I plan to cut the rug in the parlor tonight,'' Forrest said after polishing off a piece of cherry pie à la mode. ''Since my bride's getting up there in years, she finds it a mite difficult to keep up with me on the dance floor. I don't suppose you'd like to join us?''

Ruby turned to Annie. ''Forrest is a mere twelve hours younger than me and since grade school he's always accused me of being a cradle robber. He never lets up. But he's right about one thing. I just can't take the dips and spins like I used to. I'd be grateful if you could wear him down for a while after I take a turn.''

''I'd be pleased to help you, Ruby,'' Annie said.

"But I want to make sure I get a good seat for the show."

"Oh, Phillipe Nadeau is singing tonight, isn't he?" Ruby said, opening her eyes wide. "If there ever was a looker, he's one."

Forrest gave a snort. "Yeah, and every time I see his picture on the cover of one of those tabloids you bring home from the grocery store, he's got his arm around another woman. I bet he goes through women faster than he goes through shirts."

"Until the right one comes along," Ruby replied. "Then hearts will break all around the world."

"I reckon you can put your tissue away, honey. I don't see that sly one settling down in the next century. He's a rooster who's got the keys to the henhouse."

There was a catch in Annie's voice as she countered, "I bet most of the hens don't even lock the door."

"Maybe he'll ask me to dance," Ruby said to her husband. "One of the women in the beauty salon this afternoon told me he's going to dance with the passengers before the early show tonight."

"Be still my beating heart," Forrest said, theatrically bringing his hands to his chest. When Ruby slapped him playfully with her evening bag, he added, "Phillipe's dance card is probably already filled. And besides, you're with me, remember?"

Ruby rolled her eyes. "I keep trying to forget."

They're perfect for each other, Annie decided as she walked behind them into the Stardust Lounge. Forrest tugged his wife onto the dance floor and called to Annie, "Don't get lost in the crowd. I'll come lookin' for you as soon as I tucker out my bride."

Annie nodded congenially and found a vacant swivel-backed chair a few rows from the dance area. She had no sooner placed her purse in her lap when she heard a masculine voice ask, "Would you like to dance?"

Chapter Five

Annie spun around at the unexpected invitation and found the cruise director offering his arm to her. "I'd love to, Mr. Roth," she said, rising.

"Please, call me Russell." He guided her onto the crowded floor. "How are you enjoying your cruise so far?"

Annie smiled. "It's so much more than I ever expected. I envy your job. I'd love to spend a couple of months on this ship."

Russell laughed. "It *is* a wonderful job, I'll agree. But believe it or not, I look forward to my two weeks off every other month so I can go home to my family in Minneapolis."

Annie started to ask about his family when a young man with slicked-back hair tapped Russell on the shoulder. "Mind if I cut in?" he asked.

"Of course I do," Russell returned with a wounded look. "Save another dance for me," he said before slipping away to find another partner.

"My name's Tony," the man told her, reaching for her hand. She guessed he was in his early twenties, but it was difficult to tell. He was attractive enough, she noted, but he wasn't strikingly handsome—not like Phillipe Nadeau.

"Are you here with that group of teachers from Indianapolis?" Tony asked.

Annie shook her head. "I'm from Iowa. And, let me guess, you're from New York."

"Hey, this lady's a sharp one," he announced to a couple nearby. When the tempo of the music slowed and Tony placed his arm around her waist, a flash of panic shot through her. She had no idea of where to place her hands. The last time she'd danced was at Elmo's sister's wedding two years ago, and her partner was in his eighties! Annie scanned the crowd until she caught a glimpse of Ruby, whose arms were draped around Forrest's shoulders. She did the same, bringing a smile to Tony's lips.

"Would you like to sit this one out? I'll buy you a drink," he asked.

"Uh, no thanks," she returned abruptly. Feeling self-conscious, she lifted her hand from his shoulder and played with her hair. What was it with men on cruise ships? she wondered. Did they all hope to win a woman's favors by offering her a drink? Had she done something to inadvertently lead him on? She was so unskilled in social situations that she didn't know what to think. Talking with strangers at Sadie's—that she could handle. This was a whole new ball game!

When the band finished the number, Tony politely excused himself and quickly vanished, leaving Annie alone on the dance floor. She squeezed through the crowd and returned to her seat. Not a second later a cocktail waiter approached and laid a napkin on the small round table beside her.

"What can I bring you?" he asked.

"A diet Coke, please," Annie answered. The man nodded, then whisked off to another table.

At that moment Annie noticed Phillipe standing across the room. Captain Emerson was with him, as was a stunning silver-haired woman, and—Annie practically had to stand to get a better look—a gorgeous platinum blonde. She was small and reed-slender, dressed in a vivid mini-length red-sequin gown. Even from a distance Annie could see that she was holding fast to Phillipe's arm.

Annie slumped in her chair. Her instincts about Phillipe had been right. She supposed his attention would be devoted to Blondie, at least until another equally beautiful woman crossed his path.

She sighed and stared at the dazzling couple. He, dark and dashing in his tuxedo. She, opalescent and stunning in a dress that positively sparkled beneath the ballroom lights. There was no doubt about it. They made an impressive couple.

Phillipe gave the young woman a seductive smile as he suddenly wrapped his arms around her and began to sway with the music. They danced cheek to cheek and Annie doubted if a greased butter knife could have slipped between them. Resentment brought a flush to her face and she drew a deep breath. She was suddenly overwhelmed by a flood of unfamiliar and confusing emotions. Anger, jealousy, and betrayal doused her like a tidal wave.

Struggling to maintain her composure, Annie stared

at her hands and noticed for the first time a pile of shredded paper on the tabletop where her napkin used to be. Unnerved, she tried to roll the pieces into a ball, but only succeeded in scattering them all over the table. *Get a grip on yourself,* her mind screamed. How could the man's mere presence frazzle her so much?

The waiter delivered her Coke and placed another napkin on the table. Annie felt her face flame as he gathered the tattered paper in his hands. She took a long sip and tried to focus her attention on the other dancing couples.

Instead, she found herself scanning the crowd for Phillipe. When he came into view, her heart pounded and her pulse raced. She caught herself this time as her fingers made a small tear in the napkin. He was driving her to distraction! She was letting her heart rule her head, she decided as she grew more annoyed with herself with each passing second. She had to get out of here.

Annie hadn't even planted her feet on the floor when, looking up, she saw a familiar figure approaching her. The air rushed from her lungs. As she made an attempt to swivel her chair around, Phillipe caught her arm. His fingers were warm, and his touch sent a tingle through her. She attempted unsuccessfully to snatch her arm free.

"Anna, I'd like to dance with you," Phillipe told her with a smile.

"No, thank you," she answered stiffly.

But Phillipe obviously had other plans. He took her hand and slowly drew her to her feet. His dark brows grew together in a frown. "You're angry with me. Why?"

Annie hadn't anticipated a confrontation and for a moment she stood speechless. "Why?" she repeated as Phillipe drew her toward him. She pulled back. "I just don't want to dance," she said, lowering her voice to an urgent whisper because she noticed the cocktail waiter had stopped nearby and was eyeing her speculatively. "I don't dance well," she added feebly.

Phillipe merely grinned.

Before she could think of another reason, he led her deftly across the hardwood dance floor. Darn the man! It wasn't going to be easy to prove to him that she wasn't like all the other fawning women when she fell under his spell the minute he laid eyes on her. Confusion boiled within her. How could she be so completely drawn to someone who was so similar to her father? She wished she knew. *Keep your head,* a silent voice urged. *Don't look into his eyes.*

"Just relax and follow my lead," he said, sweeping her onto the dance floor. His arms cradled her as if she were a delicate flower. "I've missed you," he murmured, smiling down at her.

"You've been so busy, I'm surprised you had time to miss me at all," she replied stiffly, focusing her gaze on his chin. Flustered, she missed a step. Phillipe's strong hands tightened on her waist as she stumbled against his chest.

He laughed softly and lifted her hair from her shoulders. "An important thing to remember while dancing is to always watch your partner's eyes, not his feet," he said. "I saw you dancing with the other men. I hoped you'd save at least one dance for me."

"You weren't exactly chairbound yourself." As soon as the words were spoken, Annie bit her lip, wishing she'd kept her mouth shut. She had no claim on him.

Phillipe leaned closer and whispered, "It's flattering to know you were watching me."

"Likewise," Annie replied, feeling her cheeks tinge.

"Why wouldn't I want to watch the most beautiful woman in the room?" he said softly.

She blushed. "You shouldn't say things you don't mean."

"Ah, but I do," Phillipe assured her. "There's not a man in here tonight who wouldn't swim laps around the ship to earn the pleasure of having you in his arms."

Nor a woman who wouldn't do the same thing to trade places with me, Annie thought, aware of the admiring glances following them.

"You probably noticed that most of my time was occupied with the captain's stepdaughter."

Annie blinked up at him as his words echoed through her head. "The captain's—"

Phillipe leaned back and looked at her. "That's right. Clarissa is a bank manager from Phoenix," he murmured.

"That's nice," she returned.

His gaze held steady. "She's also engaged to a policeman. They plan to marry in February."

"Really?" Annie asked in a small voice.

"Really," Phillipe assured her.

The tempo of the music changed again and she hesitated. "Now what?" she asked, a little breathless.

"Now this," Phillipe replied, gathering her hand in his. Within seconds, Annie found herself waltzing for the first time in her life. It was surprisingly easy, she discovered, as if she had always known how to do it. They moved gracefully across the floor, as though they had spent hours rehearsing the steps. Annie felt more alive, adventurous, and carefree than she had in a long while. She basked under the warm, tender gazes Phillipe gave her and matched him smile for smile as they circled the dance floor.

Annie felt like Cinderella. She had been turned into a lovely princess and was dancing with a handsome prince in a fairy-tale land where everything sparkled and glistened and there were no worries. But lingering in the back of her mind was the realization that when this magical cruise was over, she would have to go back to her real world.

When the strains of the waltz faded and a new song began, Annie felt Phillipe slipping his arms around her waist, drawing her close. Her hands fluttered briefly before circling his neck. She closed her eyes and sent up a silent prayer that she'd always remember every second of this night. Unable to resist, she nestled her head on his shoulder.

His chest rose and fell with a deep breath. "There's a full moon tonight," he whispered in her ear.

She lifted her head to look at him, smiling dreamily. She really didn't feel like talking. It would break the spell. She just wanted to float around the room to the music and pretend she was in another world.

"Let's go outside and dance beneath the stars."

Annie's feet stopped moving. Her heart did a flip-flop. "Outside?" Her voice cracked.

Phillipe nodded, his gaze unwavering.

She gulped. "But . . . but . . . there's no music out there," she stammered, looking into his eyes.

"I could sing to you," he said with a smile.

Her fingers tightened around his shoulders. She realized she was trembling again. "Shouldn't you say something like we could make beautiful music together?"

"I'm much more subtle."

"Oh? I hadn't noticed." But Annie did notice that they were no longer dancing. Phillipe led her across the floor. Before they reached the door, she asked the obvious. "We're going upstairs, aren't we?"

Phillipe turned to face her. "Yes, we are. I want to kiss you and I'd rather not do it on a crowded dance floor." His smoky gray eyes locked with hers.

"I see." A little breathless, Annie tore her gaze from his. "I certainly can't accuse you of not making your intentions perfectly clear."

"Why not? We're both adults. We know how to communicate with each other."

Annie had her mouth open for a clever retort when she decided that now wasn't the time to challenge him. She simply nodded instead.

Without further conversation, she went with him, ignoring the inner voice that told her she was completely crazy. They climbed the stairs together hand in hand, up one flight, around a landing, up another, then another. He opened a long glass door that led to a wood-plank walkway. From there, stairs ascended to the observation deck.

The deck looked different at night, she thought. It was so dark and deserted. She cast a sidelong glance at her escort and swallowed the lump that blocked her throat. She could hear the water hitting the sides of the ship before she moved to the railing. The crash of the waves seemed weak compared to the churning within her.

She took a deep breath and looked toward the sky. The heavens shone with a million stars. "Have you ever seen a night more beautiful than tonight?" she asked.

He hesitated only an instant before answering. "It's perfect."

Suddenly Annie felt all the breath go out of her. A strange weakness fluttered through her. She tried to hold herself rigidly, not wanting to lose herself to him again.

"What's wrong?" he asked, his dark eyes probing hers.

"Nothing," she croaked, her throat suddenly dry.

"I think you worry too much," he said in a deep tone. "You need to relax, unwind, enjoy yourself."

Annie looked up at him. "For somebody who just met me, you seem remarkably certain of what I need."

"It was a simple observation," Phillipe said with a laugh.

She looked away hastily, then stepped out of his reach. Awkwardly, she cleared her throat. "Just look at those stars. Have you ever tried to count them?" Her eyes were irresistibly drawn upward.

"No," he whispered as his lips brushed her hair. She shivered at the unexpected contact.

Phillipe slipped off his tuxedo jacket and placed it around her shoulders. "You should have told me you were cold," he whispered.

Annie swallowed and shook her head. "I'm only a little cold, but I'm a lot nervous."

His eyes searched hers. "Surely I don't frighten you."

"You scare me to death," she admitted matter-of-factly.

"Why?" he persisted.

Annie shrugged, clutching the satin-trimmed lapels to bring his jacket more securely around her. It felt cool and silky and it smelled like him. It's odd, she thought suddenly, how protected she felt with him even as her heart pounded and her knees knocked. She was frightened and contented at the same time. "I don't honestly know why," she said softly.

"I have a confession to make, Anna," he said, his eyes serious as she met his gaze. "I'm a little scared of you too."

"Of me?" Annie couldn't believe her ears. What reason on earth could he have to be fearful of her?

"Look over there," he said, abruptly changing the mood. He turned her gently toward the bow of the ship and his arm came around her as he pointed to the sky.

"A falling star!" she exclaimed. "Quick! Make a wish!"

Phillipe laughed. "You can't be serious?"

She was. Annie closed her eyes, smiled, and made a wish.

"Do you do that often?" Phillipe wanted to know.

"No," she murmured, her hands gripping the brass railing. "I've only done it twice before."

"When?"

"Once from the top of the Ferris wheel at the Iowa State Fair on my thirteenth birthday and once last summer while I was walking home from wor—" Goodness! She'd have to be more careful. What would he think if he found out she didn't even own a car?

"Did your wishes come true?" he asked.

She smiled and shook her head. "Not yet."

"Ah." He lifted her hand, then examined it, palm side up. "If I were a palm reader, I'd say you're an eternal optimist." When he pressed his lips to the center of her palm, she felt a tingling sensation all the way down to her toes.

Carefully, she drew her hand away. She took a long breath and leaned on the railing.

"Do you ever think about traveling?" he asked.

Annie felt her knees weaken. How could he possibly have known that her fondest desire was to travel? "Sometimes," she answered cautiously. "Other than this trip, I probably won't go anyplace for a while."

"Where would you go if you could?"

She closed her eyes. "First, I'd go to New York City," she murmured. "I've always wanted to see the Statue of Liberty and go to the top of the Empire State Building. Then I'd fly to London and Paris. And I'd like to ride on the Orient Express." She opened her eyes. "You've done that, I suppose. Ridden on the train?"

"Yes, I've done it."

"What was it like? Did you eat a ten-course meal while speeding over the Continent?" she asked, wanting to see her wishes through his eyes. "Was the train elegant?"

Phillipe ran a hand through his hair before answering. "The cars were filled with stale smoke and I was tossed and bumped along as if I were riding in an ox cart."

Annie laughed. "You're just saying that to make me feel better."

Phillipe shook his head in denial, but his grin belied his intent. "Where else would you like to go, Anna?"

"Do you really want to know?"

"Yes, I do. Please tell me."

"Well, after I return from Europe, I'd like to set foot in every one of the states. Maine would be the perfect place to start. In the autumn, when the leaves are changing. Then I would drive all through New England and head down to Washington, D.C. I want to see the White House and Mount Vernon and Monticello. The Smithsonian would be another good place to stop, don't you think?"

"Of course," Phillipe replied. "What else would you do?"

"I'd start a spoon collection and add one from every place I go. Then I'd buy a huge, elaborately carved wooden rack to display them on. I'd hang it in the dining room of my Victorian mansion."

"Dream big, I always say."

"I suppose you think I'm being silly."

"Not at all. Where would I be now if I hadn't dared to dream?" Lightly he fingered a loose tendril of hair on her cheek. "Do you plan on traveling alone, or with someone?"

Annie sighed wistfully. "Someday I'll get married and have children. They'll go with me."

"What about your husband? Could he come too?"

"If he helped with the driving, sure, why not?" she said, enjoying his teasing mood.

Phillipe moved toward her slowly. "You're a very special woman," he said, tilting her chin and looking directly into her eyes.

She could hardly catch her breath. Why did he affect her this way? Annie always had considered herself a private person, yet after knowing this man for two days, she was sharing more of herself than she ever had with anyone.

He smiled tenderly. "I want to spend more time with you, Anna."

His frankness shocked but didn't surprise her. Phillipe Nadeau was a man who spoke his mind. And she was a woman who spoke hers. "I don't intend to let you," she responded sincerely.

"No, I don't imagine you will. But that can't stop me from trying." His voice had dropped to a whisper and she shivered. The conversation had taken a sudden turn and she wasn't sure she liked its direction.

She opened her mouth to respond, then closed it immediately as she realized she didn't know what to say. He looked at her steadily, his gray eyes holding her immobile. She blinked, trying to break the spell. But try as she might, she felt herself inescapably drawn to him.

Phillipe should wear a warning label that said, *Dan-*

*gerous. Prolonged exposure to this man could cause
serious loss of mental health*. She was behaving like
a starstruck teenager and she knew it. She should get
her feet in gear and start walking to her cabin. She
knew she couldn't, though.

Annie drew a shaky breath and pressed her hands
to his chest. "Phillipe," she protested. "I don't
think—"

"Don't think, Anna," he murmured.

"But. . . ." She should tell him that she was a waitress. *Do it, do it,* her conscience nagged. But before
she could speak the words, his head lowered and his
lips took gentle possession of hers. Her thoughts were
suddenly obliterated. Finally, he lifted his head and
stared into her eyes.

Their bodies swayed slightly with the movement of
the ship. The night air was cool, yet she felt flushed.
Entranced, she raised her hand to touch the lean plane
of his face. Loving fingers traced his smooth cheek,
stroked the rugged line of his jaw. If she lived to be a
hundred, she would never forget him. His image would
be with her forever.

"Phillipe," she murmured shyly.

"What is it, Anna?"

"I think it's time for me to go to my cabin."

After what seemed an eternity, he nodded. "I'll
leave it up to you, Anna," he said and reached for her
hand. "But it *is* only ten o'clock."

Swallowing hard, she struggled to speak. "I really
should call it a night."

Phillipe shrugged. "Or we could watch the Slim
Weaver comedy show in the lounge."

She was unable to say a word.

"Come on, Anna." He squeezed her hand, startling her with his abrupt change in tone. "Let's take in the show. And tonight's dessert night on the midnight buffet. We could go up afterward and see if we can find something chocolate."

Annie's first instinct was to make some comment about the lateness of the hour, but she caught herself in time and resisted the urge. This was the trip of a lifetime. Why should she huddle alone in her cabin and dream of what might have been? Why not live a little? And why not with a handsome man who enjoyed her company?

"Okay," she responded finally. Her practical, logical reasoning floated off to sea with the nighttime breeze. She was only getting in deeper water, she realized as he sent her a beguiling smile. Slowly her feet moved in the direction of the stairs. Perhaps she had misjudged him. Perhaps she should get to know him better.

She asked, "I told you my dreams, Phillipe. What are yours?"

"Mine?" he said as they descended the stairs. He held a door open for her and they stepped into the noisy lobby. Pulling her to his side, he whispered, "My dream is to have a long, uninterrupted dinner under a canopy of stars, dance with the accompaniment of a full orchestra, and then have a champagne toast at midnight. All with you."

"Oh, my," she said breathlessly, willing her heart to stop racing.

He flashed her a wide smile, then slipped his jacket

from her shoulders. "It's much warmer in here, don't you think?" he said.

At that point all Annie could do was nod. They walked into the darkened theater and took their seats just as the show began.

Later, they joined the milling people in the dessert buffet lines. "What are your plans for tomorrow?" Phillipe asked.

A waiter handed her a chilled plate and she smiled her thanks. "Let's see, tomorrow we'll be in St. Martin," she thought aloud. "I haven't signed up for a tour, so I guess I'll find a quiet beach and sit in the sun." She speared a giant slice of pineapple and lowered it onto her plate.

"Here, take some of this," Phillipe suggested, adding a scoop of a heavenly looking concoction beside the pineapple. "It's oranges and coconut in whipped cream with a splash of rum," he told her.

Annie eyed it suspiciously, then looked at Phillipe. "Are you having some?"

"I'll sample yours," he said.

They moved through the line, sharing a plate, taking small portions of each dessert. "I've never seen such beautiful food. It's prepared so artistically," she commented when they sat down. She thought of how Elmo marveled when he cut two carrot sticks the same length for a chef salad.

"The Tropicana Cruise Line hires only the best," Phillipe said, picking up a huge, succulent strawberry that had been dipped nearly to the stem in chocolate. "Open wide."

Annie smiled as he slid the sweet fruit into her mouth.

He grinned mischievously. "I'd like to spend the day with you. I have somewhere special in mind, and I'd like to share it." A smile lit his eyes. "We could work on making some of your wishes come true."

She nearly choked on the strawberry. What was he saying? What was he planning? Why couldn't she chew faster?

He checked his watch. "I didn't realize it was so late. I'm due in the Brass Hat Piano Bar in fifteen minutes." To Annie's astonishment, he stood. "I'll meet you in the ship's library near the purser's office at ten o'clock."

She swallowed hard. "You'll what?"

"I'll take care of everything," he assured her, bending to brush his lips across hers.

"But, Phillipe," she protested. "What about your band? Don't they need you here? You can't take off and leave them, can you?"

He touched the tip of her nose with his finger. "That's the best part of managing my own staff. I can do whatever I want." He kissed the top of her head. "And tomorrow I want to spend time with you and your freckles."

Nervously Annie ran a hand over her cheeks. "Freckles?" she repeated numbly as if in a trance. As he started to walk away, she finally found her tongue. "Are we leaving the ship? How should I dress?"

"Yes, to your first question and"—he looked contemplative—"wear something nice but casual. We'll be eating—Well, never mind where we'll be eating. I want you to be surprised.''

He wanted her to be surprised? What else could she be?

"See you in the morning," he called over his shoulder.

A shiver rippled over her. What had she gotten herself into?

Chapter Six

Annie was sitting alone in the ship's library the following morning with a cup of orange spice tea and a book when Phillipe walked through the door. She was so absorbed in what she was reading that he startled her with his greeting.

"Good morning, Phillipe." Annie smiled up at the man who'd promised to surprise her. His hair, still damp from a recent shower, fell casually across his forehead. He wore trim black slacks and a white cotton shirt. He had left the shirt open at the collar and rolled up his sleeves to reveal tanned, muscular forearms.

"What are you reading?"

Annie showed him the cover, which displayed a dark, rakish pirate and a fair maiden. "It's a wonderful book about the legends of the Caribbean." Smiling wistfully, she closed the book and placed it on the table. "I love reading stories about heroes."

Phillipe laughed. "Sounds like fairy tales to me."

"This book calls it folklore, but I call it romance."

"I could have guessed you'd be a tried-and-true romantic."

Warmth crept onto her cheeks. "Do you think so?"

"Most definitely," he said, nodding his conviction. He offered her his arm. "*Mademoiselle,* your chariot awaits."

"You've hired a chariot?"

He laughed in a deep, jovial way. "Actually, your first mode of transportation is a tender boat, then after that, well''—he grinned at her—"let's just say you'll be surprised."

The warmth of his smile and her racing heart caused Annie to wonder whether or not her legs would support her when she stood. She scooted to the edge of her chair.

"Shall we?" Phillipe prompted.

Nodding, she rose and lightly touched his sleeve. She tried to squelch her rising excitement. It simply wouldn't do for her to leave the ship with this man *and* abandon her common sense. *Shake it off, Annie*, she told herself. *Pull yourself together*. Despite orders from her sensible side, she still felt like giggling.

As promised, a bright orange tender boat awaited at the end of the gangway. "Welcome aboard, Mr. Nadeau," a white-clad ship's officer called. "The water's rough this morning, so you might want to sit in the middle of the bench."

"Thanks for the warning," Phillipe replied. He boarded first, then helped Annie on. Much to her surprise, the boat was nothing more than four rows of narrow benches with life jackets stacked beneath them.

"I hope we won't need those," she said, her eyes lingering on the orange-and-black vests.

Phillipe smiled. "Can you swim?"

"A little," she admitted, hoping he wouldn't ask

her to clarify her answer. She'd hate to confess that a six-week course in second grade was her sole swimming experience.

"I don't think you have anything to worry about." Phillipe sat down and crossed his legs in a relaxed manner. "I've planned a special day for us, and swimming ashore from a capsized boat isn't on our itinerary." Annie smiled shakily and sat beside him.

As forewarned, the ride was bumpy but fortunately brief. There was a taxi waiting when they reached the shore.

"Welcome to St. Martin," the driver said, pulling away from the curb with a lurch.

"Thank you. Princess Juliana Airport, *s'il vous plaît,*" Phillipe responded matter-of-factly.

The driver nodded, then engaged Phillipe in a conversation, both speaking fluent French. Since Annie had no idea what they were saying, she turned her attention to the scenery. She smiled in appreciation of the pastel-painted Caribbean cottages that marched down a flower-decked hillside to the ocean. All the islands had similarities but looked so different, she thought, trying to pay close attention to the details in order to accurately describe where she'd been to her friends back home.

She'd read in a guidebook that the island was divided in two parts. The French side, St. Martin, was a flurry of shops, traffic, bars, and casinos. She knew the airport was located in St. Maarten, on the Dutch side of the island.

Airport, Annie thought in alarm, when their destination finally registered in her brain. Why on earth were they going to the airport? She continued to look out the window, conscious of very little of what she saw. She toyed absently with the straps of the canvas bag sitting on her lap and tapped her foot on the floorboard. Where was he taking her?

The cab suddenly came to a brake-squealing halt at the far end of the airport terminal. "*Joyeux Noël,* Mr. Nadeau.''

"*Merci,*" Phillipe replied. He paid the driver and they got out of the car.

She took a gulp of the taxi's diesel-fumed exhaust, making it necessary for her to swallow several times before speaking. "Where are you taking me?" she asked finally in a casual tone, trying to conceal her concern.

The sizzling smile he gave her sent her pulse soaring. "I'm taking you to a magical place where fantasies come true," he answered, leading her around the side of a one-story brick building.

When Phillipe approached a small, silver plane, Annie strongly considered running in the other direction. But she knew it was too late. She had her chance to say no last night, or even this morning. But now, all she could do was live with the consequences.

"After you," Phillipe said with a sweep of his arm.

Annie put one foot on a metal step, then stopped. "I'm not sure this is such a good idea," she told him. "Maybe we should tour the island and go back to the boat. You probably have a million things to do and—"

"Anna, there is nothing more important for me to do than spend today with you." He gave her a gentle push and followed her onto the plane.

Once inside the passenger cabin, Annie noticed that there were only two plush red velvet seats. A cloud of thick, white carpeting beneath her feet matched the gleaming interior. A silver tray with two long-stemmed crystal glasses awaited them on a small stand. A bucket of iced champagne stood nearby.

They took their seats. She buckled her seat belt and pulled it snug. ''The flight will be a short one,'' Phillipe informed her. ''Only about twenty minutes.'' With practiced skill, he uncorked the wine and poured it. Then he gave her another heartwarming smile. ''Champagne?''

Annie considered declining, then decided a few sips might settle her nerves. ''Just a little, please.''

He poured the sparkling liquid. Lifting his glass, he looked deep into her eyes. ''A toast. To you, Anna. May all your dreams come true.''

''Thank you,'' she whispered and brought the champagne flute to her lips. She saw her hand shake. It was ridiculous to feel so miserable. She should sit back, relax, and enjoy the day. But she couldn't. She almost felt guilty for having Phillipe all to herself. Alone.

''Aren't you going to try it?''

Annie suddenly realized the glass was still touching her lips. How foolish she must look! She smiled weakly and took a sip. She'd never had champagne and the bubbles tickled her nose. She swallowed and decided she liked the way it felt, tingling her throat. She sipped some more.

''Do you like it?''

''Oh, yes,'' she murmured. ''This is delicious.''

Phillipe looked at her over the rim of his flute. His

eyes twinkled as if he knew a secret. It made her immediately suspicious. Annie's eyes widened when she heard the engine whirl to life. For a moment she'd actually forgotten she was on a plane. "Are you kidnapping me?" she heard herself ask, hardly recognizing her own voice.

"Would you like me to?"

"I don't think so."

Phillipe took her hand in his. "You have nothing to worry about. I'm simply taking you to my favorite spot on the island. It's a resort and restaurant called La Maison. I've often wondered if it's possible to get a bad meal there, so in the interest of research I keep going back to challenge the chef. So far he hasn't disappointed me."

Annie could only nod. Suddenly, they were in the air. She sat perfectly still. The plane ride was nothing at all like the smooth, comfortable flight from Miami to San Juan. She could only pray that the pilot knew what he was doing. When the plane bounced and her ears popped, she had serious doubts as she clutched the arms of her seat. Up, down. Up, down. Her stomach flipflopped with every rise and fall.

She ventured a peek out the window and noticed the plane was circling a small strip of grass that Annie hoped was not the landing field. It was. The runway looked about the size of a Band-Aid, and the pilot's approach by way of a low pass along the craggy cliffs of a mountain did nothing to settle her stomach. A curiously light-headed feeling crept over her, and she wondered if she might be ill. Finally, and not a moment too soon, they were safely on the ground.

A few minutes later they were strolling along a delightful butterscotch-colored beach. Annie lifted her face to the sun and smiled.

"Safe and sound," Phillipe proclaimed.

"I wasn't so sure there for a while," Annie returned. "I've never been in a plane that small."

"I didn't think you'd want to walk here. It's straight uphill for about forty miles."

"Good guess," Annie said, wondering if her voice would ever return to its normal pitch. She stopped walking, slipped off her sandals, and wiggled her toes in the powdery grains. The breeze caressed her face and she inhaled deeply, hoping it was possible to capture the scent of the ocean and hold it in her memory.

Phillipe put his arm around her shoulders as if it were the most natural thing in the world to do. Her heart lurched at his closeness. "I'm glad to see you're not the type who gets airsick," he teased.

"I guess you didn't notice," she said, looking up at him, "that I turned several shades of green up there."

His rich laugh made her skin tingle. But strangely enough, she also began to relax. "Perhaps, but no longer. You look positively beautiful right now."

Annie laughed, but was immensely pleased at the compliment. She wanted to look wonderful for him. The longer they walked, the less inhibited she became. In fact, she felt so comfortable in his casual embrace, she wished the beach would go on forever. It was almost as if they were heading down a magical path to another world.

All too soon they approached a white stucco building that Annie guessed was the resort.

"Here we are," Phillipe announced, removing his arm from her shoulders. "Just thinking about this place makes me hungry. The food here is *magnifique*." He kissed the tips of his fingers dramatically. "But, I'll admit, I'm a bit prejudiced. The owner is a friend of mine."

Annie smiled as they stepped onto the porch. A pink-and-green awning marked the entrance to the huge A-frame lobby. The door was propped open and they walked right in. She looked beyond the high-ceilinged room to the alluring lagoonlike swimming pool with gazebos that appeared to be floating along the waterside.

Suddenly, a white-jacketed man came up to them. "Phillipe!" he called. "It's about time you came back. I was beginning to think you didn't like our cooking anymore."

"You know better than that." Turning to Annie, Phillipe said, "This is Paul Thompson. Paul, this is Anna Stewart."

"How do you do?" she asked, extending a hand. From Paul's midwestern accent, she knew Phillipe's friend wasn't French as she had expected.

Paul, who had twinkling blue eyes and a friendly smile, shook her hand enthusiastically. "Nice to meet you." With a sweep of his arm, he said, "Come. I'll show you to our best table."

He led them through the main dining area, where colorful batik-print cushions brightened the wicker chairs. They continued walking and eventually went back outside to a private porch. Annie took two steps and came to a halt, staring ahead into a courtyard and beyond to the spectacular view of a waterfall cascading down a mountainside. It was absolutely breathtaking. She'd never seen anything so beautiful.

Paul held out her chair. Annie sat but continued to stare in wonderment. She reached out to touch a petal of bright pink bougainvillea that was entwined in the lacy, white gingerbread trim next to the table. Her gaze traveled leisurely around the cozy dining area, then lingered on the beach below, where about a dozen windsurfers were braving choppy seas and strong winds in their colorful crafts.

Finally, Annie looked across the table at Phillipe and saw that he was watching her. A tremulous shiver coursed through her.

"I thought you'd enjoy eating out here on the veranda."

Veranda. How exotic it sounded!

"Are you ready to try the best food you'll ever taste?" Phillipe asked, giving his napkin a snap and placing it on his lap.

"Any time you are," Annie returned. It was still early, but she'd skipped breakfast and now she was hungry.

Paul returned with a platter of mangoes, papayas, pineapple, watermelon, and, according to their host, a local delicacy called "fig" bananas. There was also fresh orange juice, a basket of warm homemade breads, and a pot of potent Caribbean coffee. *Good*, Annie thought, smelling the welcoming aroma. She suspected the champagne was contributing to her light-headedness and she hoped the coffee would anchor her feet back on the ground.

The food was wonderful, just as Phillipe had promised. When Annie thought she could eat no more, Paul arrived with lunch. "Iced gazpacho accompanied by lemon sole and crisply breaded scallops," he announced, spreading the banquet before them. To her dismay, he also brought wine.

Annie couldn't imagine such a variety of food served at a single seating. "Are we supposed to eat all this?" she whispered to Phillipe after Paul was gone.

"Indeed," he assured her. "You'd better help yourself while there's still food on the table."

Annie did just that. When the seafood was nearly gone, she put her fork down, took a sip of water, and found Phillipe watching her again. She swallowed and suddenly went still, afraid she'd somehow committed a breach of etiquette.

"Enjoying your meal?" he asked gently.

"Yes." Despite her self-conscious jitters, she smiled at him. "Why are you looking at me?"

"I was thinking how beautiful you are and how lucky I am to have you all to myself today."

Annie gulped down more water before attempting to speak. "This is the best meal I've ever eaten," she said finally.

Phillipe shook his head. "You know what that means."

She narrowed her eyes in thought. "That we don't eat anything else for the rest of the day?"

He chuckled, the throaty sound making a shiver tin-

gle down her spine. "That we come back to make sure
the chef maintains his standards."

"I'm planning to return at least once a year," Annie
teased with a dramatic toss of her head. "Perhaps I
should fly down for my birthday."

"When's your birthday?" Phillipe wanted to know.

"The eleventh of July," she replied.

He gave a decisive nod. "Then it's settled. We'll
meet here in seven months and"—he did a quick cal-
culation—"twenty days."

Annie returned his smile, hoping he wasn't serious.
She hadn't been able to afford a bus ticket to attend
the state fair in Des Moines last year on her birthday.
Catching a plane bound for St. Martin was as unlikely
as flying to the moon.

Who was she kidding, anyway? *I must not*, Annie
told herself firmly, *read more into his attentiveness
than is actually there*. And, even more important, she
must not lose sight of who she was. Phillipe Nadeau
came from a different world, a life-style beyond her
comprehension, and was definitely out of her league.
He was used to glamorous women who moved in the
fast lane. She didn't even own a car.

"You're suddenly a million miles away, Anna.
What are you thinking?"

She squirmed in her seat, trying to figure out how
to answer his question without telling the whole truth—
but without telling a lie. She decided on the truth. "I
was thinking how different we are."

His mouth curved in a beguiling smile. "I'm a man.
You're a woman. I'd say we're just different enough."
His voice was deep and soft.

Annie blushed. "That's not what I mean. We have such different backgrounds." She stopped abruptly, realizing she had revealed more than she meant to. She glanced down at the twisted napkin in her lap.

"Well, we both enjoy eating. You can't deny that. It's something we have in common."

She lifted her head and met his gaze and found it impossible not to return his irresistible smile. In spite of her misgivings about herself and her circumstances, she relaxed.

Paul brought another bottle of wine, and promptly refilled Phillipe's glass and started to pour more into Annie's, but she covered it with her hand. "No more for me, please. I lose my head when I have too much to drink."

"Oh?" Phillipe grinned rakishly. "I'll have to remember that."

"I don't drink very much," she confessed. "I prefer—"

"Warm tea," Phillipe supplied.

"Shall I bring tea with your dessert?" Paul asked her.

"Yes, please," she answered.

"What desserts do you recommend today?" Phillipe said.

"Do you have to ask?" Paul returned.

The men exchanged smiles. "I'll have the chocolate coconut cake with caramel and Brazil-nut frosting," Phillipe told his friend.

Paul turned to Annie. "And for you?"

"It sounds too fabulous not to try," Annie said with a smile.

"It's my personal favorite," Phillipe told her.

Whether it was the wine or the man Annie wasn't certain, but she suddenly felt bold. "Tell me more of your personal favorites," she said.

"I've developed a taste for Dutch apple pie and—"

Annie's laughter stopped the flow of his words. Phillipe looked at her curiously. "Not just your food preferences. I want to know more about *you*."

"As they say, my life's an open book."

"It's one I haven't read, Phillipe."

He reached across the table and covered her hand with his. "What would you like to know?"

The contact made her pause, but when he smiled, Annie decided to plunge ahead. "Well, for starters, are you from a large family?"

Phillipe shook his head. "I have parents, naturally, and a brother. But I don't spend much time with them."

"Why not?" she asked.

He hesitated, an almost pained expression on his handsome face. "From the time I was a small boy, my parents traveled a great deal. My father's company constructs bridges. He and my mother were usually off to parts unknown for months at a time."

"That's too bad."

Phillipe shrugged. "I'm sure they loved me, but the truth is, they simply had no idea how to raise children."

"Who stayed with you?"

Phillipe sighed in resignation. "My younger brother Jean-Claude and I were rather precocious. We exhausted a number of nannies over the years."

Annie smiled and shook her head. "I bet you were a real handful."

"I still am," he said with a sly grin. Then his face became more serious. "When I turned ten my parents sent me to boarding school in England. Since my brother was only six, he stayed home and they hired a governess for him."

"They separated the two of you? How awful! Didn't they realize how miserable you'd be?"

Phillipe shrugged again. "Apparently not."

"Weren't you lonely?"

"I was at first, then I made some friends. In retrospect, I now realize that my parents actually did me a tremendous favor."

"How so?" She gave him an inquiring look, hoping he'd elaborate.

Phillipe leaned back in his chair and gazed off into space. "It was January when I arrived at the Brookshire Academy for Boys. My dormitory was a dark, cold, gloomy place and I was scared. I did what any frightened ten-year-old would do—I hid." His eyes came to rest on Annie's. "I was so well hidden, in fact, it took several teachers most of the afternoon to find me."

Annie could see the haunting pain in Phillipe's eyes as he spoke, but it was the hollowness, the emptiness, the soulfulness of his expression that touched her heart. She, too, knew about loneliness. The longer she looked at him, the more she realized that he no longer resembled a superstar. "Where did you hide?"

"In the music conservatory, under the grand piano. The dean of music found me. Dean Walter Shelton." He said the name with reverence, and Annie suspected that the dean had had a significant impact on Phillipe.

"I remember looking up at his icy blue eyes and

stern face and thinking he would give me the thrashing of a lifetime.''

''Did he?''

A smile softened Phillipe's features. ''No. Instead he sentenced me to a month of polishing the instruments. While I cleaned, he played the piano. Before the month was over I was pleading with him to teach me. He did, and the rest, as they say, is history.''

''That's a fascinating story. I've never heard anyone tell it about you,'' Annie reflected aloud.

''That's because you're the first person I've ever told.''

She tried to swallow the lump that lingered in her throat. ''I feel honored.'' Tears welled within her eyes. ''Thank you for sharing it with me.''

''Thank you for listening,'' he said in a soft voice, reaching over to stroke her still-flushed face with his finger.

''Phillipe Nadeau!'' a decidedly French, masculine voice called from somewhere inside. Annie looked up to see a rotund apron-clad man dodging the tables and chairs in the dining room, heading toward them.

''Anton!'' Phillipe rose and greeted the man with a kiss on each cheek. They exchanged a few words in their native language, then Phillipe turned to Annie. ''Permit me to introduce Anton Boulinger, the most talented chef in the Caribbean—''

''*Du monde!*'' the man interrupted with a broad sweep of his arm.

Phillipe laughed. ''Excuse me, in all the world.''

Annie met the smile and the hand that was offered. ''The food was exquisite, Mr. Boulinger.''

"*Mais oui,*" he returned to Annie, then unleashed a rapid succession of words to Phillipe.

Phillipe threw back his head and laughed. At that, Anton shook his plump fist, and the men launched into another lengthy discussion. After several minutes, Anton suddenly headed back to the kitchen.

"He certainly had a lot to say to you," Annie said.

Phillipe nodded, then drained his water glass. "He challenged me to find either a better meal or a more lovely dining companion anywhere in the universe."

"Did you accept his challenge?"

"Of course," he replied. "Food and women are my two biggest weaknesses."

Annie lifted her eyebrows. "Yes. Your reputation is well known."

He waved a hand in the air. "The press likes that image. They exaggerate everything."

"Naturally, you discourage reporters from spreading rumors about you," Annie prompted.

"No, I don't," he said unexpectedly. His eyes searched her face but he didn't smile. "My image is convenient," he said. "I even encourage it."

"What?" Annie couldn't believe her ears. "You actually want people to believe you're a . . . a . . . playboy?"

"Why not? I'm single."

"But you expect me to believe you're not as much of a Casanova as everyone thinks."

Phillipe cleared his throat. "My situation is difficult to explain, Anna," he said softly. "I sing love songs. I try to create a romantic mood when I sing. People expect me to behave in a certain way. It's part of the act.'' Annie glanced away, suddenly uncomfortable, but he continued. ''Please don't make the mistake of thinking I'm everything I'm reputed to be.''

''How will I know when you're sincere and when you're not?''

His eyes caught hers and held them. He looked as surprised as she felt. Silence stretched between them. Phillipe's eyes never left hers. ''I've never intentionally hurt anyone. I never would.''

Paul walked onto the veranda with two generous slices of cake on a silver tray. He must have sensed the tension between them because he quietly set the plates on the table and discreetly left without a word.

Annie unenthusiastically raked her fork through the thick, nutty chocolate icing. Phillipe took one bite and pushed his plate aside. He gave a long sigh before reaching into his pants pocket and pulling out a small package.

''An early Christmas present,'' he said, smiling modestly. He handed it across the table to Annie.

She held the red foil–wrapped box in her palm in disbelief. For several seconds she merely stared at it. A flicker of apprehension coursed through her as her mind jumped to numerous conclusions, none of them good.

''Aren't you going to open it?''

Annie moistened her lips. ''This is so . . . unexpected.''

''I wanted to surprise you. Go ahead,'' he prompted, ''open it.''

She slid off the thin gold ribbon and slowly removed the paper. When she opened the hinged lid, she found the most elaborate pin she'd ever seen—a delicately detailed gold butterfly with tiny diamonds and sapphires encircling the wings.

She was speechless. She knew it must have cost a small fortune. *The more expensive the gift, the bigger the favor,* an urgent voice inside her warned. She placed the box on the table. "I . . . I can't accept this, Phillipe."

"Why not?" he asked. "Don't tell me you already have one."

Annie shook her head. "No," she answered, her voice tremulous. How could she explain to him that she never, absolutely never, accepted gifts from men? "I—I didn't get a gift for you," she stammered. "It would be wrong for me to take this."

"But I want you to have it, Anna. It reminds me of you. Elusive and free." He removed the butterfly from the box and pinned it on the collar of her blouse. Then he slowly brought her hand to his lips and kissed it. For a moment, his eyes held hers, and she saw a genuine warmth in his expression that touched her deeply.

Although she knew it was wrong for her to even consider accepting such a present, she sensed that Phillipe enjoyed giving it to her. She couldn't hurt his feelings, could she?

"I sincerely want you to have this," he said, bringing a blush to her cheeks.

Perhaps he simply wanted to buy her a Christmas gift—no more, no less. Perhaps she was overreacting. He'd given her no reason to mistrust him. Why was she assuming the worst? "Thank you, Phillipe," she whispered, hoping she had reached the right decision.

"You're welcome," he said, standing. "If we're going to explore the shops and make it back before the ship sets sail, we should leave. The plane will return for us soon."

Chapter Seven

A short time later Annie and Phillipe were back on the French side of the island, window-shopping. Fortunately, once again, a group of fans detained Phillipe long enough for Annie to slip inside one of her sponsoring stores and redeem her gift certificate for a set of five red leather Gucci bags, each nestled one inside another. Phillipe now carried the shopping bag containing Annie's treasures as they walked along the main street in the central business district.

"Let's go in here," Phillipe suggested, opening the door to a boutique.

"Okay," Annie said, wondering why he'd be interested in such a place. As she entered the store, the overpowering scent of incense caused her nose to twitch. Her stomach knotted at the sight of a mannequin clad in a sheer, black, lacy evening gown positioned prominently at the door.

A brisk, efficient-looking saleswoman approached them immediately. "Can I show you something?" she asked. "Perhaps something from our wide selection of swimwear?"

Annie forced a smile and shook her head. "No, I—"

She could hardly believe her ears when Phillipe interrupted and asked the woman to show them to dresses.

"Blue is your favorite color, isn't it?" he asked Annie over his shoulder as the clerk led them down the center aisle.

"Yes," she replied and quickly added, "but I really don't need any more clothes." She couldn't even afford a belt in a store like this! And if Phillipe Nadeau thought for one minute she'd let him buy her anything in this store—

"Here we are," the saleswoman said, interrupting Annie's stream of consciousness. She pulled a slinky sequined cocktail dress from a rack. "This shade of aqua will look lovely on you." She held it under Annie's chin. "You're a summer, aren't you?"

Annie had absolutely no idea what the woman was talking about. She frowned and said simply, "I was born in July."

The clerk pursed her lips in a peculiar expression. It reminded Annie of the sour face a little girl had made at Sadie's when she tried to eat the lemon from her mother's iced tea. Right now Annie felt equally sour and wanted nothing more than to escape from the saleswoman's probing eyes.

"With your blond hair and fair complexion, I'd definitely say you're a summer," the woman said decisively. With that pronouncement, she started bundling selections in her arms. "I'll start a dressing room for you," she said, racing off toward the back of the store.

"Phillipe," Annie pleaded as soon as they were alone. "The clothes in here are lovely, but I . . . I. . . ."

"I'd like to buy you something," he said, lifting a white beaded sweater from a circular rack.

"No," she replied in a low, anguished voice.

"Why not? It would be my pleasure."

Annie's stomach clenched even tighter. "You already got me the pin. I don't need anything else. Please."

Phillipe looked at her intently. "You don't like receiving gifts?"

"Sometimes I do, but. . . ." Annie chewed on her bottom lip.

"But what?"

"I already told you that I haven't gotten anything for you," she improvised, hoping he'd let the matter rest.

For a moment Phillipe didn't reply. Then he cleared his throat. "You've given me today, Anna. A day spent in the company of a beautiful, charming woman is the best present a man could receive."

But how long would he be satisfied to receive only her company? Her creed had always been to avoid men who bought expensive gifts. Phillipe had just stepped over the line. Conflicting emotions of guilt, confusion, fear, and humiliation waged war within her. How was she to react? What was she to say? Annie looked down at the butterfly pin. Elusive and free. If only he knew. "I won't let you buy me anything in here," she said firmly.

Phillipe's brows drew down in a deep frown. "Whatever you say." He thanked the bewildered clerk and they walked out onto the street.

On the sidewalk, he asked, ''Are you ready to return to the ship?''

His voice held a trace of annoyance and Annie wondered if he might demand an explanation she wasn't prepared to give.

''Yes, I'm ready.'' How could she explain that in her experience if a man bought a woman a gift, it meant she was expected to pay in a different coin?

Annie hurried along the sidewalk. To her dismay, Phillipe matched her step for step. She had to put some distance between them. The quicker they went their separate ways, the better. As soon as she could gain enough composure to string words together to make a sentence, she intended to tell him so.

Phillipe hailed a taxi. A few minutes later she sat beside him on the crowded tender boat. Taking a deep breath, she tried to focus her attention on the middle-aged couple seated across from them. When she looked up at them, they both smiled. The woman exclaimed, ''How romantic! What did he buy you, dear?''

Oh, no! Annie thought in alarm. They saw the Gucci shopping bag and thought Phillipe. . . . She pressed her knees together and straightened her back. ''It's just a purse. And Mr. Nadeau merely offered to carry it for me,'' she replied. She turned her head away from the couple, but not soon enough to miss the slow, lazy wink the man tossed at her.

Annie suppressed a moan. She had the nagging suspicion that once back on the ship, the couple would point her out to the other passengers and say, ''There's Phillipe Nadeau's newest conquest.'' That thought unnerved her to the very core. She didn't want to be yet another in a long series of women.

All the way back to the ship, she mused on the fact that fate seemed to be tempting her as it had her mother. In frustration, she gripped the edge of the tender with such force that her knuckles turned white. Silently, she vowed over and over again that she wasn't going to be like her mother. *She* knew better.

When the boat finally pulled up alongside the gleaming white cruise ship, Annie grabbed the handles of her shopping bag and hastily made her way to the exit. She ran up the gangway, flashed her boarding pass to the uniformed crew member, then stepped to one side to face Phillipe.

"Join me for a drink on the Lido deck?" Phillipe asked before she could speak.

The question sounded more like a direct order than an invitation. Annie felt her temper rise in response. She drew a deep breath and let it out slowly. "No, thank you," she countered icily.

Phillipe's eyes caught hers and held them. "Something's bothering you. Please tell me what it is."

Holding the shopping bag in front of herself at waist level like a shield, Annie swallowed hard. There were many things she needed to say to this man, yet her thoughts were so jumbled she hesitated to speak. "Nothing," she mumbled, not sounding very convincing.

She felt as if his dark gray eyes could see right through her. "Are you ill?"

"No." She sighed and turned to look out at the shimmering water.

"Anna, what have I done to upset you?"

"I've had a wonderful day with you. I really appreciate everything you've done for me."

He brushed the tip of his finger across the bridge of her nose. "If it was such a wonderful day, then why is there a rain cloud frowning on your freckles?"

His abrupt change in mood caused Annie to look up at him. He'd mentioned her freckles again. She knew that dozens of the pesky brown dots were probably sprinkled across her face. Even the briefest exposure to the sun encouraged them to multiply. No doubt her face was positively polka-dotted after walking along the beach.

He'd done it again! Phillipe had turned on the charm and her brain had ceased to function. Freckles were the least of her troubles. Her honor was at stake. Nervously, she moistened her dry lips and stared into his beguiling eyes. How on earth would she muster the courage to say thanks but no thanks? She simply wasn't interested in exchanging favors with him.

She closed her eyes for a moment, took a steadying breath, and then ventured a peek up at him. A slight frown creased his brow. *Stay calm,* Annie told herself. She could handle this.

"Anna, there's something wrong and we have to talk about it."

She started to voice another denial, but Phillipe already had his hand on her arm and was leading her through the lobby. He swept her around a corner into a narrow corridor, stopped abruptly, and turned to face her.

Annie let the shopping bag slide from her fingers.

It landed with a muted thud on the floor. Not knowing what to say, she stared at it.

"Your mood changed the moment we walked into the boutique," Phillipe said quietly. "Please tell me what's wrong." He lifted a finger to push back a tendril of hair that had fallen across her cheek.

She found his gaze disturbingly intense. Nothing in her life had prepared her for the overwhelming way she'd been affected by Phillipe. She was disillusioned, confused, and nervous beyond belief. She rubbed her hand across the bridge of her nose, fighting the impulse to tell him everything. But that was impossible. Yet maybe there was some way she could explain some of her feelings. She had to say something before she exploded. "I . . . I feel uncomfortable when men offer to buy me things."

"All men or just me?"

"All men," she answered with conviction.

Phillipe's eyes narrowed. "Why?"

Annie shrugged. "I can't tell you."

"Try."

Her lower lip trembled as she returned his stare. "All right. I'll tell you. I simply don't want to feel obligated to you."

Phillipe looked surprised. "Excuse me?"

"Everything you've done for me had been so wonderful, so unexpected. But now I feel"—she paused, searching for the right word—"indebted to you. It makes me uncomfortable."

"I'm confused, Anna. Have I ever asked you for anything in return?"

"No."

"But you think I will."

"I think you *might*."

Phillipe rocked back on his heels. "So you don't trust me, is that it? You think I have an ulterior motive."

"I don't know you very well, Phillipe, and I don't feel right about your buying me things." Annie said each word slowly, with precision.

Phillipe's eyes widened. "I thought all women liked men to pamper them."

"Many women probably do. But this woman doesn't," she replied, folding her arms protectively over her chest.

"Forgive me if I've offended you," he said, studying her intently. "I make a great deal of money and if I see something I want, I buy it."

"Do you always assume people are going to go along with your whims?"

A dark expression crossed his features. "Taking you to the resort today and buying you a gift wasn't a whim."

"My point exactly!" Annie looked down at her hands. "Phillipe, I don't want to hurt your feelings. I'm sorry if I have." She raised her eyes. "I told you before that you scare me. You still do. And right now, I'm even scared of myself."

"Why can't you accept that what's happening between us is genuine?" he asked.

Annie exhaled in frustration. "Because there's a lot you don't know about me."

"That's because you haven't told me." His finger

tenderly traced the line of her cheekbone and jaw. "I never intended to frighten you. I am who I am."

She stared at her shoes. "I guess I've never met anyone quite like you."

"I probably take some getting used to." He gently lifted her chin with his finger. "Can you overlook my dozens of faults and be my friend?"

His friend? He wanted her to be his friend? Annie looked at him, unable to answer right away. She could offer no logical explanation why she shouldn't be. He had been kind, caring, and generous.

He gave her a small smile and reached out to clasp her hands. "Today was very special to me."

"It was for me too," she whispered. The realization of just how special made her shiver slightly. What was it about the man that made her so wary? She already knew the answer. She was attracted to him, more so than she had been to any other man.

"Tell me something," Phillipe said, his smile direct and engaging. "If the stars were out right now, what would you wish for?"

"Oh, I don't know—" she said, drawing back slightly.

"Pretend," he urged, cutting off her protest. "Pretend we're standing on the highest deck and the night is filled with a thousand stars. You have one wish. Anything in the world. Tell me what would make you happy."

She took a deep breath and closed her eyes. "I'd wish that today would never end. That we could stay exactly the same as we are right now, and live hap—" She caught herself before she said too much.

"Anna," he said, squeezing her hands. "Do you know what I like best about you?"

She opened her eyes and shook her head. "No. What?"

"You're honest. That's a quality I admire greatly. You're also not afraid to dream."

Annie cocked her head to one side. "I've been accused of having my head in the clouds. I guess it's a childish trait I'll never outgrow."

"I hope you never do. I find it charming."

Annie was about to make a comment when a group of teenagers turned into the corridor.

"Oh! Mr. Nadeau!" a girl with curly dark hair gasped. When Phillipe turned toward her, she smiled shyly.

"*Bonjour, mesdemoiselles,*" he returned. "Did you enjoy your day in St. Martin?"

None of the girls answered. They stood as stiff as statues, staring at him adoringly.

"I'll be singing in the disco at four-thirty. I hope I'll see you there."

From all the smiles and nodding, Annie was sure the group wouldn't miss it. Phillipe wished them well and the girls nearly swooned as they squeezed past.

"Now, where were we?" he asked Annie. "If I remember correctly, I was complimenting you." He smiled, and she felt her pulse soar. She was no better than the teenagers. Feeling embarrassed, she looked away. What was it about the man that caused her heart to beat so fast?

"Now that you've told me, I won't make the mistake of trying to buy you anything."

"Thank you," she whispered, feeling warmth settle on her cheeks.

"You're not angry with me now?"

"No," she said, releasing a pent-up sigh.

"Friends?" Phillipe prompted, holding out his hand.

His look was so sincere that Annie couldn't have resisted had she tried. "Friends," she agreed, grasping his strong hand.

Phillipe tucked her hand into the curve of his arm. "Come on. I'll walk you to your cabin."

"I wasn't planning on going to my cabin right away."

"Oh?"

"I finished the novel I was reading and I'd like to stop by the gift shop and look for another one."

"Great idea. I'm on the last chapter of mine so I might as well go with you." He picked up the shopping bag and they walked back through the lobby. "If memory serves me correctly," he said, pushing the down button on the elevator panel, "the gift shop is on the Riviera deck."

"Do you enjoy reading?" Annie asked, trying to digest this new information about the singer.

"Of course, why shouldn't I?"

"I . . . I never thought. When do you find time to read?"

"Morning, afternoon, evening. On airplanes, between shows, before bed." He held the elevator door for her. "It may come as a surprise to you, but I read several books every month. When I was at school in England, I acquired a deep affection for Sir Arthur Conan Doyle."

"You're kidding! You read mysteries?"

"And science fiction and adventure. And biographies—I love biographies. I also like to work crossword puzzles."

Annie opened her mouth to say she did as well, but just then the elevator stopped, and a crowd of boisterous men got on, pushing them back into a corner.

After an interminable elevator ride, they finally reached the Riviera deck. Annie and Phillipe let the noisy mob get off first before they so much as looked at each other again.

Phillipe was the first to speak. "Unless I miss my guess, that crowd spent their afternoon on the *Mama Fumba Rumba*."

"What on earth is that?"

"It's a glorified cattle barge with a few deck chairs and an enormous bar. It circles slowly around the cruise ship for a couple of hours."

"Who on earth would get off a cruise ship to ride around on a barge?"

Amusement flickered in his eyes. "Men, that's who." At her look of confusion, he continued. "For twenty dollars, you and your fellow passengers are served bottomless rum drinks and treated to an exotic performance by Calypso dancers. They drink and watch until the world slowly recedes. Then they crawl back onto the cruise ship and pass out."

"You made that up!"

Phillipe, looking sober and sincere, crossed his heart. "I never lie."

"How do you know so much about the *Mama Fumba Rumba?* Could it be from firsthand experience?"

Phillipe feigned a stricken pose, but his eyes sparkled with merriment. "*Moi?* Certainly not. I simply read the advertisement that was slipped under my door this morning."

Seconds later, and still grinning, he and Annie went into the gift shop. She headed toward the circular rack of romance novels while he browsed through the adventure section. Both made their selections quickly and met at the cash register. When Phillipe laid a chocolate peanut-butter candy bar on the counter, she stared in disbelief. He actually ate something they sold in the diner! Common, regular food—who would have thought?

"Please ring the books separately and include the candy with mine," he told the cashier, then grinned at Annie. The woman responded with a broad smile and spoke to him in Spanish. Annie stared at Phillipe in bewilderment as they conversed for several minutes, drawing giggles and a blush from the clerk.

"Are you ready?" he said at last.

She nodded woodenly. "You speak Spanish as well as French?"

"*Sí,*" he returned with a wink. "I also know a few words in German, Portuguese, Italian, and one other language—oh, yes, English."

"Don't you get the languages confused? I mean, don't you ever say the wrong thing?"

Phillipe laughed. "Most definitely. It seems around you I've acquired a habit of always saying the wrong thing."

"Fortunately, I'm a forgiving person," Annie teased, trying to keep the conversation light.

When they turned to walk down the deserted corridor toward her cabin, he reached for her hand. "I wish I could spend time with you this evening, but tonight will be rather long for me. I'm scheduled to do three shows and I'm afraid it will be impossible to slip away."

"I understand," Annie replied, struggling to keep the disappointment out of her voice.

"Would you like to meet tomorrow for lunch?" he asked. "If we make it for around two o'clock, we should be able to have some privacy."

Annie shivered at the word *privacy*. The thought of being alone with him for even a short amount of time sent her emotions reeling. She mused at the fact that Phillipe thought it was going to be a long evening. Well, it wouldn't be half as long as hers without him.

It was at that moment that she realized the extent to which she had allowed him to occupy her thoughts and her time. A little more than three days ago, they'd never even met. Now she felt depressed at the prospect of not seeing him for a few hours.

At her cabin door, he kissed her cheek. Then his hands tightened around her waist. He leaned his head down and rested his forehead on hers, looking into her face. "You're very hard to resist, Anna," he whispered.

She gave a little laugh. "So are you."

His lips returned to her cheek and trailed softly over to her mouth. "Perhaps someday you'll find me irresistible," he continued, now nibbling at her neck.

She felt his hands slide through her hair and watched, mesmerized, as his lips descended to meet hers. Annie lowered her eyes, helpless against the flush that spread across her features. Then panic surged through her. For the first time she realized what her mother must have felt with her father, and Rick's father, and with all the other men whose names Annie had lost track of.

Twisting in Phillipe's arms, she tried to free herself. What had come over her? she wondered, not sure how their friendship had progressed so far so quickly. Probably because she had let it. She'd better say something fast, while she still could. But what?

"Phillipe," she whispered, still breathless from his kiss.

"Yes?" he asked, loosening his grasp slightly so that he could look into her face.

She couldn't meet his eyes. "I can't think when you kiss me," she said in a soft voice.

"Are you asking me not to kiss you again?" he questioned, releasing her with a sigh.

Annie shivered. She suddenly felt cold and abandoned, and wished she could snuggle back into his arms. "I don't know what I want," she answered quite truthfully. "I think it might be a good idea if we didn't spend quite so much time together."

He took a deep breath, his face drawn and taut. "If you're sure that's what you want," he said softly.

She felt hot tears burn in her eyes. Anger would have been much easier for her to take. Instead, his gentle words and the injured look in his eyes tore at her heart.

"It is."

"Well, okay then."

Annie turned to face her door and fumbled through her purse until she produced her passcard. ''Good-bye, Phillipe,'' she murmured without turning around.

''*Adieu,* Anna,'' she heard him reply.

With numbness spreading from her brain to her feet, she walked into the cabin and closed the door behind her.

It was over. She had shut Phillipe Nadeau out of her life.

Chapter Eight

Phillipe closed his cabin door and leaned against it. How had he let his life get so complicated? Lifting a hand to the back of his neck, he massaged his tight muscles. It was no wonder he had a massive headache. He hadn't had a decent night's sleep in two days.

It was his own fault, as was his inability to keep Anna Stewart out of his thoughts. He needed her in his life like the Caribbean needed more water. No, he silently affirmed, walking over to the bed, she definitely wasn't his type. He eased onto the mattress and kicked off his shoes. The whole situation was absurd. Impossible. Insane. He'd be far better off without her.

Who was he kidding? The shaky, uneasy feeling that vibrated his insides had nothing to do with the fact that the ship was now in motion. What bothered him was the prospect of not spending any more time with Anna Stewart. But why?

Although his contact with her had been brief, he found himself strangely attuned to her. He recognized an affinity between them, and he *was* attracted to her— more attracted than he had been to anyone in a long, long time.

He sensed the attraction was returned. Yet he'd never met a woman who tried to deny it more. What was it about her that mesmerized him so? Was his curiosity piqued by the challenge of a woman who didn't chase him? Even as the thought crossed his mind, he knew it wasn't true. He liked her. It was as simple—and as complicated—as that.

And why couldn't she accept his generosity? He had money. He liked to spend it. And he'd like to spend it on her. But he couldn't. She'd made that perfectly clear. She didn't want to feel obligated to him. What had Anna been saying, really saying? It sounded so simple, yet the hidden message was something deeper, more personal. If he had to guess, he'd say that someone had hurt her very badly in the past, and she was afraid of getting hurt again.

He sighed and rolled onto his side. What was the matter with him? He handled the whole situation with the finesse of an adolescent. For somebody reputed to be worldly and sophisticated, he was doing a great job of discrediting himself. He couldn't remember the last time he'd failed in such a spectacular way with a woman, or wanted to succeed so badly.

The loud jangle of his telephone propelled him off the bed and across the room to the small writing desk in the corner. "Hello," he mumbled into the receiver.

"What are you doing in your stateroom at this hour?" Blake Emerson asked in his customary commanding voice.

Phillipe smiled and slid into a chair. "Are you doing a room check, Captain?"

"Yes, as a matter of fact, I am. I've been looking

for you. Will you be joining Annie Stewart for dinner this evening?''

Startled, Phillipe asked a little too quickly, ''Why do you ask?''

''I saw you and Annie get off the tender boat together.''

''You don't miss much, do you?''

''She's a lovely woman, Phillipe.''

''Yes, she is.''

''Also an engaging conversationalist, from what I hear.''

Phillipe didn't respond.

''She's getting to you, isn't she?'' Blake asked in a concerned voice.

Phillipe dragged his fingers through his hair. ''Yes, she's getting to me.''

''Do you want to talk about it?''

Phillipe drew in a deep breath and let it out. ''I don't know, Blake. She has some old-fashioned notions that I can't seem to talk her out of.''

''In other words, you can't charm her.''

Phillipe cleared his throat. ''That too. She also has a problem accepting gifts from me. And now she's decided she's better off without me.''

''So what are you going to do?'' Blake asked.

Phillipe put his hands behind his head and stared at the ceiling. ''I don't know. I just don't know. I hadn't planned on a woman like Anna Stewart entering my life.'' He swallowed. ''Is it possible to meet a woman and know almost immediately that there is going to be something very special between the two of you?''

''That's the way I felt about Pamela. I knew the first

time I met her I wanted to marry her," Blake responded. After a moment, he continued. "But you're not talking about marriage, are you?"

"No," Phillipe confessed.

"Not all women are like Leslie," Blake reminded him.

"I know that," Phillipe countered. "Anna's like no woman I've ever met. She's clever and naive, confident and self-conscious, inviting and resisting. All at the same time!"

"You've got it bad, my friend. It sounds like there isn't much not to like about her." A beeping sound came through over the line. "I've got another call," Blake explained. "I'm going to put you on hold for a minute."

Phillipe stretched his legs and closed his eyes. With the receiver tucked between his cheek and shoulder, he thought about his friend's words. What wasn't there to like about Anna? He suddenly realized that he liked everything about her—the way she smiled and the way her eyelashes swept down when she blushed. He liked the exquisite bright blue color of her eyes. He started to think about the delicate pinkness of her lips. He remembered what it had felt like to kiss her.

He sat up straighter in the chair. Anna Stewart was unique, all right. How many women carried themselves with such an inherent air of pride, identified the dialects of strangers with unerring accuracy, and recommended home remedies? She was an enigma, all right, this contest winner from Iowa.

She'd make somebody a good wife.

The thought somehow unnerved him. Experience

had taught him that permanent relationships rarely worked, and the few that did rarely worked well. His own disastrous attempt at marriage was a prime example.

He and Leslie had been introduced by a mutual friend, and they had married a month later. In the beginning they had truly cared for each other and both had tried to adjust. Then, as the years passed, both discovered they wanted different things for themselves and had different expectations of each other. Leslie no longer accompanied him on his lengthy road trips. More often than not she wasn't there when he came back home.

The press had called it an amicable divorce—no long court battle, no hostility, no bitterness, no passion. It almost seemed a natural extension of their marriage. The next step. The final step. Although he knew a marriage without love was hopeless, signing his name on the divorce papers hurt him more than any physical pain he'd ever experienced.

Phillipe heard two quick beeps and knew his friend was back on the line.

"Sorry for the interruption," Blake said. "That was the chief engineer in the radio room. We're all set for those ship-to-shore phone calls for your staff on Christmas morning. I'll have three extra officers monitoring the lines."

"Thanks for all the extra effort, Blake. It's important to me."

"You're a good boss, Phillipe."

He chuckled softly. "Some of my band's family

members wouldn't agree with you. They'd rather have my people home for the holidays.''

"That brings me to my original question. Are you free for dinner?''

"I am.''

Blake cleared his throat. "I don't know if that's good or that's too bad.''

"Anna doesn't want my company.''

"She's crazy.''

"I agree,'' Phillipe said decisively.

"That's the spirit. Dinner will be served at eight. My table in the restaurant. I'll have an extra chair just in case.''

"Thanks, Blake.''

"No problem. See you then.''

Phillipe replaced the receiver and returned to sit on the bed. He leaned forward, resting his elbows on his knees. What should he do about Anna?

Tomorrow they'd be in Guadeloupe. He'd planned to do some Christmas shopping and to take Anna with him. He realized that while it wouldn't be wise to see her right now, he could still let her know he was thinking about her.

With renewed energy, he sprinted across the room, reached for the phone and rang for the bell captain.

A loud pounding noise woke Annie. She opened her eyes and stared for a moment at the seascape on the far wall of her cabin, giving her sleepy mind time to remember where she was. When she realized that she was still on the cruise ship, delight turned up the corners of her mouth. Then the memory of her parting from Phillipe two days before intruded.

Her smile faded.

A knock on the door halted her thoughts. In a panic, she thought it might be him. "Just a minute," she called. Hurriedly, she reached for her white satin robe at the foot of the bed and slipped it on over her matching gown. "Who is it?" she asked through the locked door.

"Room service, Miss Stewart."

"I didn't order anything."

"Well, somebody ordered something for you."

When she opened the door a room steward brushed past her, carrying a tray. Annie could see that it contained a china teapot, a covered bread basket, a cup and saucer, and . . . a single white rose in a crystal vase.

"There's a card beneath the vase," the young man explained, setting the tray on the dresser. "Enjoy your breakfast." He stepped back out into the hallway and softly closed the door behind him.

With unsteady fingers, Annie lifted the vase and brought the flower to her face, burying her nose in the rose's velvet petals. The perfumed aroma reminded her of the islands, particularly St. Martin and the lovely resort, and the veranda and Phillipe. She returned the vase to the tray and picked up the card.

Her name and cabin number were printed across the envelope in precise, well-formed letters. The white card inside read simply, *I'm thinking of you. Phillipe.*

"I'm thinking of you, too, Phillipe. So much that it scares me," Annie whispered.

In fact, the entire time she'd spent at the beach on Guadeloupe the day before, she'd done little else but think of him. Today she'd stay so busy she wouldn't have a second to regret that Phillipe wasn't with her.

For the rest of the morning, Annie forced herself to participate in the shipboard activities. Since the ship was scheduled to be at sea all day, she had dozens of options. Right after breakfast, she played shuffleboard with Forrest and Ruby, until Ruby's sunburn became bothersome. Then the cruise director taught her trap shooting, and she shot at clay disks hurled off the stern of the ship by a machine. Just before lunch she took an ornament-making class and crafted a bird-in-a-nest creation for the ornament-exchange party to be held that evening.

She ate a fruit salad from the poolside lunch counter, then stretched out on a chaise longue with a crossword puzzle book. After fifteen minutes she tossed her pencil and the book into her canvas bag, no longer able to concentrate.

At two o'clock she threaded her way through the crowd assembled by the pool for a limbo contest. Although she had no desire to enter the competition, she was curious to watch how others squeezed their bodies under a pole suspended mere inches above the ground. As she chose a position to observe, she congratulated herself for not thinking about Phillipe for at least, she glanced at her watch, twenty minutes. If only she could keep this busy for the next two days.

A round of applause turned her attention to a small platform where, much to her dismay, Phillipe stood, microphone in hand.

"Who's ready to limbo?" he asked the crowd. Several women squealed their enthusiasm and quickly joined him. Annie watched Phillipe smile and talk with the other passengers. Her eyes widened when a very pretty brunette in a silver strapless bathing suit flirted outrageously with him. Jealousy stabbed at her heart. Her reaction was ridiculous, she told herself, but she felt better when the silver bombshell's boyfriend took her by the arm and escorted her to the contestant line.

Annie's gaze lingered on Phillipe. He wasn't wearing his customary tuxedo, but a white polo shirt bearing the cruise line logo. Unfortunately, Annie thought, releasing a pent-up sigh, the shirt only emphasized his broad shoulders. Now that he had walked squarely into her line of vision, it was impossible to focus her attention on anything else.

She shivered slightly and closed her eyes. She found herself picturing Phillipe reaching out to her, coaxing her to come to him. She could almost feel the intensity of his gaze upon her. The sensation was so real that when she opened her eyes she wasn't surprised to find him staring directly at her.

For a few seconds she remained frozen to her spot. Finally, her brain got the message to her feet that she should be walking, quickly. She scrambled through the crowd and up a flight of stairs to the observation deck. She slid into a chair, closed her eyes, and tilted her face to the sun.

It was impossible to banish Phillipe from her thoughts. That realization led her to another: Despite her best intentions, she'd fallen in love with Phillipe Nadeau.

Dinner, as usual, was a delightful event. The Italian food was scrumptious and, thanks to the Greenes, the conversation was lively. The waiters had entertained the passengers with a song-and-dance routine to the music of "Rudolph the Red-Nosed Reindeer." Yet despite the friendly atmosphere and abundance of holiday cheer, Annie wasn't in a festive mood. She was about to excuse herself and return to her cabin when she realized she'd stayed a moment too long.

Phillipe had entered the room.

She'd learned how to recognize the signs of his presence. The room suddenly quieted to a low hum of hushed voices. A wave of whispers fluttered in the air.

Even without turning around, Annie also knew when he stood behind her. The spicy clean scent that had become so familiar surrounded her. Gently placed fingertips grazed her shoulders, pressing the cool, silky material of her dress to her skin and sending a shiver down her spine.

"Good evening, Anna."

She drew in a fortifying breath before swiveling in her chair to face him. In a white tuxedo jacket and red silk tie, he looked magnificent. *Get a grip on yourself,* her mind implored.

"Hello, Phillipe," she managed in a choked whisper. "Do you have the evening off?" Why had she asked that? She felt the color rising on her cheeks.

"As a matter of fact I do." He gave her a smile that sent her pulse racing. He turned to face the Greenes. "I don't believe we've met. I'm Phillipe Nadeau."

"Howdy," Forrest replied. Annie finished the introductions. Phillipe shook Ruby's hand first, then Forrest's.

"I'm delighted to meet you, Mr. Nadeau," Ruby said. "Can we persuade you to join us for dessert?"

"They're serving those little rolled pastries called cannoli with cream on the inside and chocolate sauce on the outside," Forrest added.

Phillipe held up his hands in mock surrender. "You just said the magic word. Chocolate. I'll stay." He sat down next to Annie. "So you two have had the pleasure of dining with Anna this week," he said, placing a napkin in his lap. "Tell me, did she guess which part of the country you're from?"

"Yessiree," Forrest returned. "Right outta the hatch she had us pegged as Texans. She's a sharp woman, no doubt about it."

The compliment caused Annie to blush. She stared at her hands, wondering how she could change the subject. Before she could think of something suitable and safe, she heard Phillipe clear his throat and ask, "What do the three of you have planned for this evening?"

Thankfully, Forrest spoke up. "Well, it being Christmas Eve, the missus and I are going to mosey up to the tree-decorating party in the lobby. Then, I suspect we'll dance for a while, and at nine we'll watch the tree-lighting ceremony."

"We didn't put up a tree at home this year," Ruby explained. "The purser told us the crew has spent all day putting up lights and ornaments on over twenty trees on the Promenade Deck."

Phillipe nodded. "There'll be trees on display from several countries. Yvette, the casino cashier, and I decorated one from France.'' He turned to Annie. ''What about—''

''Boss!'' Randy rushed up to their table. ''Excuse me for interrupting, but we have a small crisis.''

Phillipe stood and asked quietly, ''It's not Nadine again, is it?''

Randy shook his head. ''It's Stuart, the flutist. He's had the hiccups for the past two hours and the band's due to perform in less than twenty minutes.''

Phillipe raked his fingers through his hair. ''Has he tried fresh air?''

''He's tried everything,'' Randy confirmed. ''He's blown into a paper bag, gagged down a gallon of water, and held his breath till I thought he'd keel over.''

''Has he tried eating ice cream?'' Annie asked in a small voice.

''Ice cream?'' Phillipe repeated.

Annie nodded. ''Eating a bowl of ice cream has been known to cure hiccups.''

Phillipe look dubious. ''Any particular flavor?'' he wanted to know.

''Strawberry has always worked for me,'' she told him. ''But I imagine any flavor will do.''

''I think spumoni is on the menu tonight,'' Forrest provided.

''Then by all means order a double scoop of spumoni ice cream for Stuart,'' Phillipe said. ''He's been practicing 'Silent Night' every chance he's had ever since we got on board. It's his first solo number and he's probably got a case of stage fright.''

Randy gave a salute. ''Aye, aye, Boss.'' He started to walk away, then turned around abruptly. ''By the way, I noticed you'd already stacked the gifts for everybody under the tree in the practice room. I hope that just because you asked us not to buy you anything doesn't mean you aren't coming to the party.''

Annie could have sworn she saw a blush creep up Phillipe's neck. He cleared his throat. ''I'll be there, Randy.''

''Glad to hear it.'' He saluted again and was on his way.

Phillipe returned to his chair. ''Another crisis taken care of.'' He stuck two fingers in his shirt collar and twisted his tie.

Annie noted his peculiar behavior. This was a side to Phillipe she had never seen before. She had always assumed he was the master of confidence. Tonight, he appeared downright flustered. ''Tell me, Anna,'' he said, tugging down his jacket sleeves. ''Where do you come up with these home remedies?''

She shrugged with deliberate casualness. ''I watch what other people do in similar situations and learn what works and what doesn't.''

''That's fascinating,'' Ruby said. ''The advice you gave me this morning to get rid of my sunburn really worked.''

Forrest laughed. ''Yeah, but you still smell like a pickled egg.'' He turned to Phillipe and gestured across the table. ''Anna over there told my dear, sweet spouse to take a bath in vinegar.''

''Vinegar!'' Phillipe shook his head. ''You told her to bathe in vinegar?''

Annie slumped in her chair, feeling a little foolish.

"I always heard it was the best cure for sunburn," she said, carefully keeping her voice steady.

"And you were absolutely right," Ruby said. "She even suggested I ask the chef for the vinegar. Sure enough, he was more than willing to give me a gallon."

"Chanel it ain't," Forrest said, patting his wife's hand. "Speaking of remedies, I read somewhere that if you make up a potion of equal parts of brewer's yeast and yogurt and spread it on your face, it takes care of wrinkles."

Ruby slapped his hand playfully. "I suppose you're referring to your own wrinkles, old man."

Forrest grinned. "Naturally, my dear." He turned to Phillipe and launched into a story about an oilman who raised camels in east Texas. The men seemed to have a number of stories to tell and enjoyed sparring with each other. Dessert was served and, much to Annie's relief, they continued talking. She was barely able to concentrate on their conversation. One thought occupied her mind. What was Phillipe doing here?

Forrest's laughter pulled her from her reverie. "That's a good one," he said, slapping his knee. "Say, did you know that ancient people believed moonlight is helpful in fertility?"

"Oh, Forrest, behave yourself!" Ruby scolded. "Discussing fertility, of all things!"

Forrest looked properly chastised and displayed a pitiful, downcast expression. "I was merely repeating what I'd heard, Ruby."

She snorted. "Anna, don't listen to a thing he says."

"Don't be too hard on him," Annie said with a

laugh. "Many people believe the moon has magical powers."

Forrest beamed. "See, I was right. Go ahead, tell my wife all about it."

"Well," Annie said in a lowered voice. "Lunar influence is considered beneficial in removing warts."

"Good for you, Anna. I think you set him straight." Ruby stood, laughing. "My horoscope must have given me lunar influence today because right now I'm going to remove this old wart so you young people can have the table to yourselves." She held out her hand to her husband. "Let's go, Mr. Greene." Ruby smiled at Phillipe. "Please don't hold me accountable for any of the lies this ornery critter has spread."

"I wouldn't think of it," Phillipe said, laughing.

Forrest winked and took his wife's hand. "I hear there's a full moon out tonight," he whispered over his shoulder as he and Ruby walked out of the restaurant together.

Phillipe looked amused. "What a couple. I'd say those two were made for each other."

"I agree," Annie said quietly. She was suddenly very aware that Phillipe's hand was resting on the arm of her chair. Had he been sitting that close the entire time? No, she reasoned. He had moved closer.

"You haven't told me your plans for the evening." He brushed his fingertips across her knuckles, then his hand relaxed, resting lightly on hers.

Panic settled into her bones. Part of her knew that she was being ridiculous, but she didn't want to be alone with him. "Phillipe," she began, "you've probably got a million things to do and I'm awfully tired, so why don't we just say good night?''

Phillipe shook his head and didn't let go of her hand.

She frowned, glanced away, then looked back again. ''It was nice of you to join us for dessert. I'm sure you made Ruby's day.'' His gaze searched hers. ''I really should be getting back to my cabin now. . . .'' Her words trailed off as his grip on her hand tightened. She was suddenly afraid he wasn't going to let her go. Awkwardly, she cleared her throat. ''So, have you eaten dinner?''

''Yes.''

''Do you want to check on Stuart?''

''No.''

''Would you like more coffee?''

''No.''

His monosyllabic responses were getting to her. She sat up straighter in the chair and tugged at the hem of her dress. Now she was fidgeting! *Go ahead,* her mind screamed. *Cut to the chase. Ask him why he's here.* She cleared her throat. ''What brought you into the restaurant?''

''You,'' he said softly, taking her hand into his again.

Annie swallowed with difficulty. ''Isn't the band expecting you to sing with them?''

''No.''

''Why not?''

''It's Christmas Eve. The band can play without me for one evening.''

''Oh.''

"Anna, there's a reason I'm not performing to-night."

"There is?"

He nodded. "I didn't want you to be alone on Christmas Eve." He leaned over and placed a feather-light kiss on her cheek. "Will you come with me to the tree-lighting ceremony?"

She gazed up at him, touched by his invitation and by the sincerity of his words. How many men would have been sensitive enough to realize that she dreaded spending this Christmas Eve alone, more so than any of the others in the past? And, she realized, there wasn't a man alive with whom she'd rather share an evening. "I'd love to, Phillipe," she said, linking her fingers through his. "Thank you for thinking of me." She could feel herself blushing. Why did he have to be so darned charming?

He held out his hand. "Shall we?"

"So, tell me more about your staff party," she said as they walked from the restaurant.

Phillipe squeezed her hand. "Whenever we're on the road, or as the case may be, at sea, during the holidays, we all get together for a family-style dinner on Christmas Day. The night before, we exchange gifts."

"But you don't want anyone to buy gifts for you."

He shook his head. "I knew that wouldn't get past you. I get more pleasure from—" He stopped mid-sentence and cleared his throat. "Some of the band members, like my sax player, Dell, have been with me since the beginning. They're like family to me."

Annie nodded. "I can understand that." Sadie and

Gus were closer to her than her own half-brother. "You really love your work, don't you?"

"It's my life," he said simply. "The irony of it all is that success is often its own punishment. The more successful I've become, the less freedom I have. Someday I'll concentrate on more personal matters and leave the globe-trotting to the younger generation."

"Younger generation! You're hardly ancient."

Phillipe smiled and held a door open for her. "Sometimes I feel like I've been in show business forever. Someday. . . . Well, just someday," he murmured, letting the words trail off.

Annie and Phillipe entered the lobby just as the passenger ornament exchange was getting under way, precluding any more conversation. She pulled her contribution from her purse and gave it to the cruise director, who attached a number on it and placed it beneath the tree. After they sang several carols, Phillipe asked Annie if she'd mind if he spent some time at the staff party. He offered to meet her in the disco in plenty of time for the tree-lighting ceremony.

Annie enjoyed the ornament-swapping game with the other passengers. She was pleased to receive a delicate blown-glass ball with a Christmas tree inside, which she carefully wrapped in tissue paper and tucked in her purse. Her spirits were high when she arrived at the disco an hour later. However, coming alone presented her with a new set of problems.

The heavily spiked punch coupled with the fact that most of the people in attendance were college-age males brought her more attention than she thought possible. After declining many invitations to dance, one stocky young man with a peeling sunburn still persisted.

"You know, babe," he said, grabbing her arm, "I'd really like to dance with you."

Annie shook her head. "I don't want to dance right now, thank you," she returned, raising her voice above the level of the music to be heard.

The man only tightened his grip and smiled at her. "I wouldn't pass up the chance to be with Joey, if I were you." He squinted his eyes and winked. "Who knows, you might just get lucky."

"Thanks but no thanks," Annie returned firmly. "I'm waiting for someone and I'd prefer to be alone." She yanked her arm free of his grasp.

Joey caught her wrist before she could turn away. "Don't act so high and mighty, princess. You shouldn't be so quick to turn down my company. Don't knock it till you try it."

Annie tried desperately to think of a way to get rid of him without creating a scene. The man had clearly had too much to drink, and would be difficult to handle. "Excuse me," she said finally in a polite voice. "I really have to go."

"Not so fast. Give me a kiss first," the man slurred. He pulled her toward him.

Chapter Nine

Annie struggled to free herself from his embrace. After wrestling with him for a few seconds, she felt his arms go slack.

"Is this man bothering you, Anna?"

She whirled around to face Phillipe. "Yes, he is."

Holding Joey firmly by the collar, Phillipe stared down at the shorter man. Joey had sobered up considerably. "I . . . I just asked her"—he took a gulp of air—"asked her to dance."

A uniformed member of the ship's staff appeared beside Phillipe. "What's the problem, Mr. Nadeau?"

"This gentleman needs an escort to his cabin," Phillipe replied through clenched teeth.

"I'll take care of it personally." The officer spun on his heel, dragging Joey with him.

Annie released her breath in a puff of air. "I'm glad you came when you did."

"So am I." He fingered a tendril of her hair. "Come on. Let's walk outside." Annie nodded in agreement.

Once out beneath the stars, they strolled past several couples until they found an unoccupied place at the railing. Phillipe combed his fingers through his already

141

windblown hair. He leaned against the railing and turned to face her.

Silence stretched between them, but she couldn't think of anything to say. Phillipe continued to look at her, his expression unreadable. Annie saw his chest rise and fall as he drew a deep breath and let it out. He reached for her hand, caressing her fingers before bringing them to his lips.

Annie felt a chill that had nothing to do with the temperature. "Phillipe—"

"Anna—"

"You go first," she prompted.

A slow smile tugged at his lips. "I want to continue seeing you, Anna." He spoke softly, his fingers tightening over hers. "We only have two more days and I want to spend them with you."

"I'm afraid, Phillipe," she whispered. Her throat was dry and her mouth felt like sand. "Something's happening between us that I don't understand." She pulled her hand from his, threaded her fingers together, and stared at them.

"I don't understand it either," Phillipe murmured. "But I'm willing to spend as much time with you as it takes to make us both understand."

Annie looked up at him. "As you said, we only have two days," she reminded him. He smiled easily.

"Forty-eight hours."

"You're willing to devote every minute of both days to me?" she asked in what she hoped was a teasing tone.

"Yes, I am." He flashed her a grin that escalated her heart rate.

How could she disagree when she wanted so desperately to be with him? They had tonight and a pair of tomorrows. It wasn't long, but it would have to be enough. She'd denied herself one day already. It was her turn to smile. "Are you ready to join the crowd downstairs?"

"Not quite." He reached for her hands and brought them to his chest. "Before we go, I thought you might be interested in testing another remedy."

"Oh?"

Phillipe took a step, bringing them closer. "According to a doctor quoted in a Roman newspaper, kissing is good for your health and will make you live longer."

"You made that up!"

"*Au contraire*. The doctor explained that kissing stimulates the heart, which gives more oxygen to the cells."

Annie tilted her head boldly. "I'm suddenly feeling very light-headed, Mr. Nadeau. I believe I'm in need of some oxygen."

"I'll take care of it personally," Phillipe murmured.

"I liked the Victorian tree from England the best," Annie said, then took a sip of eggnog from the cup Phillipe had handed her. She licked the thick, sweet drink from her lips. "Which one was your favorite?"

"I'm partial to the French tree," he returned with a wink. "What would you like to do now? The observation deck may be too cool for you without a sweater." He leaned forward and lowered his voice. "I'm sure we could find a place that's warmer."

Annie's pulse pounded. "How about the theater? They're showing *White Christmas* with Bing Crosby."

Phillipe shook his head. "I watched it on the monitor in my cabin this morning."

"You did?" Annie couldn't imagine him doing something as commonplace as sitting alone in his room watching television. Maybe he wasn't alone. Annie placed her empty cup on the tray of a passing waiter. "It's been a long day. I think—"

"It's Christmas Eve," he interrupted. "Surely you don't want to go to bed at eleven o'clock." He gripped her elbow and Annie found herself being gently steered toward a brightly lit doorway, from which she could hear laughter.

The casino! Up until now, Annie had only peered in through the glass doors. She'd heard stories from truckers who had lost their shirts in Las Vegas. Since she hadn't a penny to spare, she certainly had no intention of gambling. The door swished closed behind her. Admittedly, she was curious how the games were played. She supposed it might not hurt to watch—from a distance.

"What would you like to play?"

Her eyes widened and she looked at Phillipe's smiling face. "I'd rather just—"

"How about the slots?" he interjected, leading her to a machine at the end of a row. He gestured to a high-backed stool. "Have a seat."

Annie shook her head. "I don't feel very lucky."

"Just play for fun, then."

Play with money for fun? Who was he trying to kid?

Annie took a step back and clutched her purse with a determined grip. "No thanks."

Phillipe's brows narrowed. "Is this your first time in a casino?"

Annie nodded.

"Well, then, you're luckier than you thought." He offered her a sudden, arresting smile. "It's an old European custom that when a man has the privilege of escorting a woman into a gaming establishment for her first visit, he also must stock her chips, or in this case, her coins. Hold onto this machine. I'll go buy you some tokens."

"No! Wait!" Her protests didn't stop him. It looked as if she was going to participate whether she wanted to or not.

Annie settled herself on the well-padded stool. Her stomach fluttered and her knees quivered. *Stop shaking*, she pleaded to herself. It wouldn't hurt if Phillipe bought her a roll of quarters, would it? She shouldn't feel guilty if he spent ten dollars on her, should she? After all, it was a custom . . . or was it?

Phillipe returned quickly with two rolls of coins. He broke the seal and deposited the money into a large white plastic cup. "Ready?" he asked, placing his hand on the small of her back.

The contact made Annie shiver. "What do all the pictures of fruit and numbers mean?" she asked in an effort to focus on something other than the warmth of his strong fingers splayed across her thinly clad skin.

"Every machine is a little different," Phillipe began. His words came from just above Annie's right ear and sent a tingle of sensitivity through her. "This is a dollar machine. You can play with one, two, or three dollars at a time.''

"Three dollars!" Annie gasped. "For each turn?" She could scarcely believe it. Three dollars was a generous tip at Sadie's Place, one she had to earn over the course of an hour. She couldn't imagine people wasting their hard-earned money.

Phillipe promptly deposited a trio of coins into the slot. "Pull," he instructed.

It was his loss, Annie reasoned as she pulled the lever toward her. "A pair of watermelons and a bell," she said unenthusiastically. "Did I win anything?"

Phillipe chuckled. "Not this time. If the bell had been another watermelon, you would have won sixty dollars.''

"Sixty dollars!"

"That's right." He pointed out the combination, which was displayed on the machine. "Any triple of bells, watermelons, plums, oranges, or cherries played with three coins wins sixty dollars. One coin nets twenty and two gives you back forty.''

"What if I get bars?''

"Well, any combination of three bars pays the same as the fruit. But if you're lucky enough to pull three triple-lined bars, the machine pays up to a thousand dollars.''

Annie stared at the colorful display in front of her, trying to digest this information. "So the more money you put in, the more you could potentially win.''

"That's about the size of it," he said, depositing more money. "Try again.''

"Two cherries and a plum." The sound of jingling

coins brought a smile to her face. ''Any pair of cherries pays out fifteen dollars, right?''

''You're a fast learner. Do you want to quit or would you rather reinvest your winnings?''

Annie bit her bottom lip. Fifteen dollars was a lot of money. Still, it was fifteen dollars she didn't have when she walked into the casino, so if she lost it, she wouldn't really be out anything. Should she go ahead and do something uncharacteristic and probably a little unwise? Other women probably did things like this all the time, she told herself. *Splurge,* her more reckless side urged. ''I'll put in a few more coins,'' she told Phillipe.

Over the next half hour, the pile of money in her tray slowly dwindled. She really should stop before she lost it all, her practical side counseled. ''One more pull,'' she said resolutely. Her heart stopped beating as one, two, three bars slid into a straight line across the machine. The red light on top flashed and the combined sounds of ringing bells and splashing coins sent Annie leaping from the stool. ''I won! I won a whole tray!''

''Congratulations!'' Phillipe said, hugging her excitedly. ''I'll go get a stack of containers to hold your money.''

''Hurry! The tray might overflow!'' she called after him. Annie stared in disbelief as coin after coin fell from the machine. With trembling fingers she took a cup from Phillipe and scooped up the warm coins, all the while feeling as if some fairy godmother had just waved a magic wand over her.

Suddenly the bells stopped ringing and a buzzer

sounded. "What's that?" Annie asked in alarm, hoping this wasn't a mistake.

"The machine ran out of money," Phillipe told her. "Just sit tight. The casino manager will be here in a minute and trade your coins for bills."

Annie nodded woodenly when the manager counted ten crisp hundred-dollar bills and placed it in her outstretched palm. A thousand dollars. Rick's tuition money for his last semester with a little left over. Maybe she'd have enough to apply as a down payment on a used car. She'd always dreamed of owning her very—

"Are you ready to try your luck at blackjack?"

"What?" Surely he was kidding. She opened her purse and tucked the bills safely inside between her wallet and sunglasses case. And there the money would stay until she deposited it into her savings account. No amount of enticement would tempt her to part with that amount of cash!

"You seem to have a knack for winning with my money," Phillipe said, helping her from the stool.

His words paralyzed her. "Oh!" she gasped. "It *was* your money. You paid for the roll of coins." She swallowed. "I guess you're entitled to the prize money."

"No, no, no," Phillipe admonished, shaking his head. "When a gentleman stakes a lady, it would be dishonorable for him to accept any of her winnings."

"Really?"

"Really," he assured her. "Now, since you've never played blackjack—"

"Who says I've never played?"

"Have you?"

Annie smiled and nodded, not revealing that she was educated by a group of truckers who dealt her into their game during an ice storm a few winters ago.

"What are you waiting for? With your luck, you'll probably hit twenty-one every time."

"I've had enough excitement for tonight, Phillipe. Why don't I watch you play?"

They walked together to the cashier's box. He slid a bill under the window. "A stack of singles, please."

The woman smiled and handed him a generous amount of white chips. Annie followed him to a felt-covered table where two men and a woman dealer were just finishing a round. Phillipe laid down a chip. "Cards for the lady, please," he said smoothly, gesturing for Annie to take a seat.

"Oh, no. I couldn't—" Annie began.

"Say, aren't you the woman who busted the bank on that dollar machine?" the man to her left asked.

Annie lowered her eyes and nodded.

"And she's about to show you how blackjack is played," the dealer said. "Place your bets."

The men did as they were told and the game was under way. Annie peeked at her card in the hole. Ten of hearts. The exposed card was the seven of diamonds. What had Hank told her? Take a hit if you hold less than seventeen? "I'll stay," she told the dealer.

The man on her right went over, but the man on her left drew a nineteen, beating the dealer's pair of nines.

"Try again," Phillipe said, depositing another chip.

Annie did. She continued to play, and the stack of chips in front of her grew steadily. Both men left and

Annie now played alone with the dealer. She was growing weary and knew it must be well after midnight. "This is my last hand," she told Phillipe. "I really am getting tired."

He nodded and slid a hefty stack of her chips across the table.

"You want me to bet *all that*?" Annie couldn't believe her eyes. There must be fifteen chips on that pile. Fifteen dollars was too much to bet on a single hand. But it was too late to change her bet. A card was already placed in front of her.

Annie took a deep, sustaining breath and tried to calm herself. She looked up and blushed furiously when she realized the dealer was waiting patiently for her to look at her lower card. Slowly, she lifted up the edge. It was the ace of hearts. The card showing was the jack of diamonds. That was blackjack! Annie nearly screamed it out.

Annie closed her eyes, too nervous to watch the dealer turn over her card.

"You did it!" Phillipe exclaimed, clamping his hands around her waist and lifting her from the stool. Annie opened her eyes as her feet touched the floor. After a moment of stunned immobility as the realization sank in, she threw her arms around his neck and kissed him soundly on the lips. His mouth was soft and warm under hers and for a few seconds she forgot they weren't alone. When a group of onlookers began to whistle and clap, Annie recovered her memory.

"We'll celebrate later," Phillipe whispered in her ear. He guided her toward the cashier's window.

"Cash her in, please," Phillipe said to the tuxedo-clad man behind the window.

"Certainly, Mr. Nadeau. We'll need some information from her, however. It's ship policy, you understand." Phillipe nodded.

"Miss, what's your social security number?"

Although she wondered why it was necessary, Annie recited the nine-digit number.

"You'll also need to sign a winnings voucher." The cashier provided her with the form and a pen.

Annie looked up at Phillipe, and at his nod she signed.

"Would you like to deposit all or part of your winnings into our vault?" asked the man.

"Oh, that won't be necessary," Annie said with a slight laugh. "Cash will be fine."

"Cash?"

"Is that a problem?" she asked.

"I'm not sure," the man said. He scratched his head. "Most people don't like to carry that much on them."

Annie eyed the towering stacks of white plastic chips. She estimated there were several hundred. Granted, she'd never had more than fifty dollars in her purse at any given time, until tonight, but she knew it wasn't unusual for others to carry much more. "Okay," she began, trying to compromise. "How about half in cash and half in a cashier's check?"

The manager turned to Phillipe. "Sir?"

Phillipe looked at Annie. "For security reasons, I think the vault is your best option. Why not take a thousand in cash and leave the rest?"

"A thousand in cash?" she repeated.

"If that isn't enough, make it five thousand," Phillipe returned.

"Five thousand? Exactly how much have I won?"

The cashier laughed. "You've won a little over twenty thousand dollars."

Twenty thousand dollars? Annie's mouth opened and closed again. "There must be some mistake." That was more than she could make in several *years* of waitressing. "Are you sure?" she whispered.

"Positively," the casino manager assured her. "You just cashed in a whole bagful of hundred-dollar chips."

"Hundred-dollar chips?" she repeated numbly, then turned to Phillipe. "I thought you said they were singles."

"They were," he said with an amused grin on his face. "They were worth a single hundred apiece."

"You mean that last hand . . . I bet . . ." she said, swallowing, "fifteen hundred dollars?"

Phillipe nodded. "You also won three thousand. I thought you knew."

Annie shook her head and the room suddenly began to spin. She saw bright lights flashing in front of her eyes. The sounds of the noisy casino ceased, then everything went black. The last thing she felt was a pair of strong arms supporting her.

As Annie slowly regained consciousness, she blinked and opened her eyes. A crowd of onlookers was gathered in a circle, all peering at her face.

"Please step back. She needs air," she heard Phillipe say. Annie closed her eyes again. She hated making a scene like this in front of so many people.

"Anna, can you hear me?" he whispered, gently pushing her hair away from her face.

She opened one eye and nodded.

"Do you think you can sit up?"

She nodded again. Feeling like a complete fool, she struggled into a sitting position.

"Take some deep breaths," Phillipe urged.

"I'm fine, really," she said. "Could we go outside for a few minutes?"

With a single movement, he swept her into his arms. "Put me down," Annie protested. "I feel ridiculous enough as it is." He smiled down at her, obviously choosing to ignore her plea. People stepped aside as he carried her through the casino.

"Wrap your arms around my neck," he said after thanking a man who held the door open for them. "We're about to go up the stairs."

"You can't carry me. . . ." She soon learned that he not only could but did carry her up two flights of stairs. Upon reaching a secluded area of the observation deck, he lowered her gently onto a canvas chair.

Trepidation added to the chill of the night air and she trembled. Phillipe slipped off his jacket and drew it around her shoulders. "Just relax," he murmured.

She closed her eyes, feeling overwhelmed. She'd never fainted in her entire life. And, of all the wrong times to do it, she had to pick tonight. Sophisticated, worldly women didn't pass out at the sight of twenty thousand dollars. Phillipe must suspect she wasn't everything she had pretended to be.

The moment of truth had arrived.

For several agonizing moments she stared mutely at

him. Her gaze slipped away and turned to the ocean. The water splashed and foamed below her, churning with the same turbulence she felt inside. Why couldn't the evening have passed uneventfully? Why couldn't she have taken her secret off the ship with her?

When she told him, what would she see in his eyes? Disappointment? Disgust? She didn't think she could endure either. Her palms began to sweat. And to think, only a few minutes ago she considered herself a lucky woman. How wrong she had been.

Get it over with, she implored herself. *Tell him the truth*. With quiet steps, Annie got out of the chair and walked to his side. She kept her eyes focused on the water. "Phillipe, I have something to tell you."

"Is it so awful that you can't even look at me?" He slid his arm around her waist and pulled her close. His fingers felt the tension that coursed throughout her body. "What's wrong, Anna?" he asked gently.

When their gazes locked, shame washed over her. She wished she could run, but his soul-probing eyes held her in place.

"This week, for the first time in my life, I had the chance to live in a dream world." She looked down at her hands and continued in a rush of words. "I know it was wrong for me to mislead you into thinking I was someone who really belonged on a cruise ship. After I got to know you, I was too embarrassed to say"— she paused and drew a breath—"I'm a waitress who works at a truck stop diner along the highway in the middle of Iowa."

Phillipe didn't bat an eye. "And you won the trip from a cereal company," he added easily.

"What!" she gasped. "You've known all along?"

"Yes. From the very beginning."

"But how . . . who . . . why. . . ."

He gently placed his fingers across her lips, halting further words. "It's not important who told me or why."

"You've known all along," she repeated in a low, tormented voice, "and you've said nothing? I'll bet you got a real hoot out of watching me make a fool of myself."

"I'm not laughing, Anna."

She backed up and planted her hands on her hips. "Does everyone on the ship know I won the trip?"

"Not unless you told them."

"Or you." Annie glared at him. He was leaning against the railing, arms folded across his chest.

"I've told no one." In a single stride he narrowed the short distance between them and placed his arms on her shoulders. He looked directly into her eyes. "Captain Emerson told me about you because I am the major stockholder in this cruise line."

"What! You own the boat?"

Phillipe released his grasp. "In a manner of speaking, yes. That's why it was important for me to sail on the maiden voyage."

Annie tried to digest this new information. One thing still wasn't clear. "Was the captain afraid I'd fall overboard or something? Did he think I'd act like some country bumpkin and offend the other passengers?"

"No, no. He wasn't worried that you'd be offensive. Blake and I were thinking about your safety. We were concerned that you might. . . . How can I phrase this so you'll understand?''

His patronizing expression said much more than his words. Humiliation and anger mounted within her. ''I understand everything perfectly clearly, Mr. Nadeau.'' As she spoke, her breath burned in her throat. ''You and the captain thought I needed a keeper, so you graciously volunteered for the job.'' A hot tear rolled down her cheek. ''I don't need a chaperone and I don't want to play any more of your games.''

She spun on her heel, but as she started to walk away Phillipe took her arm. ''Wait just a minute. I'm not the one who's been playing games. You deceived *me,*'' he reminded her.

''I had a good reason to.''

''Oh? Did you think I am such a shallow person that if you told me the truth I'd cast you aside?''

''What else was I supposed to think? Where do servants fit into your categorizing system?'' she shot back.

''I've never thought of you as a 'servant,' Anna,'' he protested, bitterness clouding his eyes. ''Is that what your charade was all about? All because of a stupid comment I made about women?''

Her stomach knotted and she stiffened under his intense glare. ''In part, yes. That's one of the reasons I didn't tell you, but that's not the point.''

''What is the point?''

Anna took a deep, frustrated breath. A wayward breeze picked up a strand of her hair and whipped it across her eyes. She pushed it aside. ''The point is, you led me to believe I meant something to you when all along you've only been paying attention to me out of some misplaced sense of duty.''

"You're calling *me* deceptive?"

His chiding hit its mark, pricking her conscience. "It seems we both took turns deceiving each other."

"Anna, maybe I *was* trying to protect you, but—"

"Protect me! What I really needed was someone to protect me from you!" Annie snatched Phillipe's jacket from her shoulders and thrust it at him. She swallowed hard and bit back tears. "I hope I wasn't too much of a burden."

"You weren't." His voice was cold, so cold that she shivered in response. "In case you're concerned about your casino winnings, I arranged to have the money deposited in a security box in the purser's office."

The money. Annie hadn't given it another thought. Heaven help her, maybe she *did* need a keeper. "Thank you," she whispered. Phillipe merely nodded.

She collected her purse from the canvas chair. With as much dignity as she could muster, she stepped around Phillipe, leaving him standing alone on the deck beneath the star-spangled sky.

Chapter Ten

Although Annie spent the day in paradise, she had an utterly miserable Christmas. She skipped breakfast and boarded the first tender boat to St. Croix. She spent all of the morning and most of the afternoon huddled beneath a beach umbrella, watching the surf pound the sand. And thinking. Memories rippled through her mind like wind on water.

She returned to the ship, ate dinner alone in her room, then packed away her clothes, her prizes, her heart.

At nearly eleven o'clock that evening the ringing phone jarred her from a fitful sleep. Who in the world would call her? she wondered, crossing the room to answer it. At least at home she didn't have to put up with bothersome phone calls in the middle of the night. It rang again before she tugged the receiver from the wall.

"Hello," she mumbled, hoping to make it clear to the caller that she had been asleep.

"Anna, I need to talk to you."

"Phillipe." She had fully expected never to hear from him again. She swallowed. "What do you want?"

"I want to talk, but not on the phone. Not like this. I'd like to see you." His voice came deep and soft.

"Now?"

"Yes, now. Right now. Where would you like to meet me?"

What could he possibly want? Annie wondered. She knew from experience he usually got what he wanted. He'd given her the chance to name the place. She'd better do it. "I don't think it's a good idea for you to come to my cabin."

"I agree. Were you asleep?"

"No," she said flatly, staring at the glowing red digits of the alarm clock as she had done so many times before. "Do you realize what time it is?"

"I do." Annie heard him swallow. "Time is running out for us. I want to see you again. Please."

The urgency in his voice surprised her. "I can meet you in the Stardust Lounge in fifteen minutes," she said.

"Until then," he replied.

As Annie replaced the phone, a thousand questions raced through her mind. Could he have missed her? Would he ask her for her address? Did he want to stay in touch with her? Did he feel any of the same strange, wonderful, frightening, confusing things about her that she felt about him? Or did he just want to say good-bye?

She pulled on a tropical-print jumpsuit, swept her hair away from her face, and secured it with a pair of seashell barrettes. She brushed her teeth, then hurried upstairs.

Phillipe was waiting when she arrived. He didn't

utter a word, but indicated that she should follow him. He led her down a long hallway, opened a black-painted door, and flicked a switch. A soft, dim light hovered over the room. "It's more private in here," he said, closing the door after she walked in.

"Where are we?"

"This is the practice room. We had our last performance earlier this evening so everything is packed up and ready to be hauled off the ship." He pulled two folding chairs off a towering stack, opened them, and placed them side by side. "Let's sit down. Did you have an enjoyable day?"

"I've had better."

Phillipe drew a deep breath and let it out again. "I know my phone call must have surprised you. We didn't exactly part on friendly terms."

"No, we didn't."

"I've missed you."

"I missed you too."

Phillipe shoved his hands into his pockets. "Anna, I never have trouble talking to women. But with you, I can't . . . I just can't seem to get the words out."

"Would you rather talk to me some other time? In the morning when we've both had some rest?"

"I can't rest." He sprang from the chair and walked to the piano. He pulled the cover over the keys and drummed his fingers on top, then turned to face her. "Since I've met you I've scarcely been able to sleep at all. Every time I close my eyes, you're there."

"I'm sorry," she whispered.

"Don't be," he said, walking toward her. He stopped at the edge of her chair, knelt down, and took her hand into his. "Anna, I can't let you walk out of my life."

Annie's heartbeat raced as she stared into his intense gaze. He wasn't joking. He wasn't flirting. He was serious. Warmth spread from her stomach to her face as the possibilities of the future passed through her mind. Would he ask her to marry him? How should she respond? She shouldn't even consider it, she told herself. Yet, the answer *yes* pounded within her. No longer able to hold it inside, the word "yes" escaped from her lips.

She stared at him in anticipation of the question she longed to hear. This was a moment she'd remember for the rest of her life. She could almost hear herself retelling it to her children and their children. The night their father proposed on bended knee, in the middle of the Caribbean in a deserted practice room of a cruise ship. He took her hand and said. . . .

"How important is it for you to stay in Iowa?"

Startled by the question, Annie slanted him a curious look. "Pardon?"

"Iowa," he repeated, getting to his feet and taking his seat on the other chair. "Do you like living in Iowa?"

"That's where my job is."

"Do you enjoy your job?" Phillipe asked evenly, his voice void of any emotion.

Annie stared at him warily. He certainly was beating around the bush. Could he be as nervous as she was? Perhaps he needed a little encouragement. "I could be persuaded to quit my job."

He took her hand in his. "I'm delighted to hear that."

"You are?"

Phillipe nodded and released her hand. "I'm not handling this very well. Please, bear with me."

"Are you trying to ask me something?" she whispered.

He released a pent-up breath. "I don't want this to be our last night together."

"Neither do I."

"I want you to come with me to Europe."

Annie stopped breathing, waiting for him to say more. When he didn't, she asked, "And?"

"And, I want you to accompany me on my tour."

She froze. "And?" she asked, hoping against hope that she had misinterpreted his message. "Are you asking me to marry you?"

Phillipe reached over and slid his hand through her hair. "Anna, I. . . . No, Anna, I'm not."

"You want me to be your mistress?" she cried, leaping to her feet.

"I want you to be my companion. There's a difference," Phillipe said soothingly.

"Not in my book there isn't." Annie tossed her hair over her shoulder in a gesture of impatience. "I knew it! I knew this would happen. Right from the beginning I tried not to get involved with you. I fought what was happening between us. I knew better than to trust you, but I didn't listen to my own common sense. Now I'm listening. Good-bye, Phillipe Nadeau." She turned on her heel and started to walk away, then she heard him get up and almost instantaneously felt him clutch her forearm.

"Don't go. Think about what you're giving up. I want you to be a part of my life."

"I just bet you do," she agreed bitterly, trying unsuccessfully to free herself. "Do you think I'm that desperate? That stupid?"

"I never imagined you'd react this way. I'm sorry I've upset you, but you can't run away from me like this. Not now. We have to talk."

"I think you've said enough," she said, fishing in her purse for her passcard. "There's nothing more to discuss."

He gently pulled her closer to him and embraced her with a tight hug. "I care about you. Do you believe that?"

"I used to." She drew back. "But not anymore." He frowned. "Just because I'm a waitress doesn't mean I don't have any self-respect or pride."

"I've always treated you with respect."

Annie nodded solemnly. "You did until just a few seconds ago."

"Do you always become angry when a man tells you that he wants to be with you?" he asked, searching her flushed face.

"Did you honestly expect the idea of becoming your 'companion' to thrill me?" She glared at him. "If you thought for one second I'd jump at the chance, then you don't know me at all." Anger simmered in her veins. She controlled it with a supreme effort of will.

"Then tell me. Help me know you."

"No."

Phillipe surveyed her flushed features and appeared to come to a quick decision. "You're confused and very annoyed with me," he said.

"Good guess," she said sarcastically.

"There's no need to be emotional over this. That's the very thing I'm trying to avoid. Emotions." He paused and took a gulping breath. "We're both adults. You're how old? About twenty-five?"

"Twenty-four," Annie said, wondering where all this was heading.

"And you've been on your own for a long time."

"Since my mother died a week after my high school graduation," she provided cautiously. "I've supported myself and my half-brother since then."

"You've worked so hard. Would it be so awful to live with a man who genuinely wants to take care of you?"

"Yes!" Annie sucked in an indignant breath and swung around. She found him studying her with far more than just a hint of pain in his eyes.

"We're running out of time together," he said very quietly. "I don't want to let you go."

"But you have no intention of getting emotional over it?" she countered.

Phillipe's smoky eyes narrowed on her speculatively and he crossed his arms over his chest. "I've seen too many men make fools out of themselves over women. I'm too old for that."

Annie slanted him an appraising look. "You're what, thirty-five? Forty?"

"Thirty," he ground out.

"Obviously you're too old for me."

"Our age difference isn't the issue. I want you to join me on my tour."

"If you want a faithful companion, get a dog!"

"I want you, Anna."

"You're a selfish man."

"That very well may be. But I won't live through another divorce. When I discovered my wife had been cheating on me, I wanted to die. Even the best relationships don't last forever," he replied. "Living together can benefit both people if they are honest with each other and keep their emotions out of it."

Annie stared at Phillipe disbelievingly. "You can't be serious!"

"I am," he assured her with cool certainty.

"You're suggesting a relationship without emotion?" Annie asked incredulously. "I've never heard of something as ridiculous or as coldhearted. How can you possibly stand there and say you intend to take, and take, and take from me without any thought of giving me anything in return?"

"What about companionship and kindness?" His gaze pinned hers.

"What about love, Phillipe?" she asked, causing him to scowl. "I expect my life partner to love me with all his heart and not be afraid to show his emotions," she said precisely.

He sighed in exasperation. "Your romantic notions are fine as long as a man and woman are content to stay together." He stared over her head, his face set in that same cool, unsmiling mask she'd seen the night before. "What happens when one or the other is no longer satisfied? Are you prepared to deal with the painful emotions that go along with divorce?'' His words were laced with bitterness.

"If two people love each other, really love each other, divorce is hardly a consideration. Look at Forrest and Ruby. Do you think they're on the verge of divorce?''

Phillipe lowered his eyes and shook his head.

"You bet your sweet life they're not. They're playing for keeps and I respect them for that. Solid marriages are based on commitment, Phillipe. And they can work as long as both partners love enough to stick with it, through good and bad, no matter what.''

"You expect a lot out of your men,'' he said.

"Correction,'' Annie replied. "Not men, man. As in one man for the rest of my life.''

"You were right about one thing. On the day that we met you told me you weren't like other women. You sure aren't.''

"Thank you,'' she said icily. "You couldn't have given me a better compliment. Now if you're finished flattering me, I want to go back to bed.'' She started to walk away.

"You're different for a reason, and I want to know why.'' His words halted her in midstride.

"What?''

He came to stand beside her. "Whether you want to admit it or not, I've gotten to know a few things about you this week. I sense there's more to your unwillingness to come with me than your notions of romantic love. I want to know your real reasons. Has a man ever hurt you?'' His eyes searched hers with an intensity she found unbearable.

Annie wanted to look away, but she couldn't. She knew Phillipe had the ability to read more from her eyes than she ever intended him to know. It was useless to pretend his feelings were unjustified.

"Anna?" he prompted, sliding his arm around her. Clearly, he was not willing to let the matter rest. "Please," he urged, his gaze holding hers. "It's important to me."

Annie stared at him, unable to answer right away. It was important to her as well. It was something she had never told anyone. Ever. She had harbored her painful memories for so many years she wasn't sure she could talk about it. It was a hurt that scarred her deeply, one she had lived with for as long as she could remember. To talk about it now, particularly with Phillipe, was something she wasn't certain she could do.

She pulled from his embrace and turned away from him. Memories of her childhood, ones she thought were long since buried, flooded her mind, engulfing her in sorrow. Her throat constricted and she blinked back tears. "I've never let a man hurt me," she said quietly. "Because I saw too many hurt my mother."

"Anna." The word came out in a whisper.

"I've never discussed this with anyone," she whispered. "I don't know why I feel the need to talk about it now."

"Perhaps it's because no one else cared enough to listen."

Annie swallowed hard and turned to look at him. He was right. There had never been anyone special for her. She stared again at Phillipe's beautiful dark eyes and handsome face. She drew in a cleansing breath and released it slowly. "It's a long, sad story."

"I have all night."

Annie sighed. "All right. I'll tell you. My mother was a cleaning woman for a wealthy man," she began quietly, unable to drag her gaze from his. "He paid her generously and gave her gifts. She was young and foolish, and she thought he loved her. He promised he'd marry her, but he never intended to. She was left on her own, expecting me. When her family found out, they turned their backs on her too. She wasn't even eighteen." Annie paused, aware of the frozen expression on Phillipe's face.

She broke from his eye contact, walked a few steps, and looked off into the shadows of the room. "After I was born my mother continued to work as a maid. She couldn't get a better job because she hadn't finished high school. But she was beautiful, and there were other men. They gave her gifts and a big line." Annie squeezed her eyes shut, trying to block out the haunting memories. "One bought me my first and only bicycle. Mom always believed they were going to marry her. They never did. They all broke her heart—and mine too. I wanted so much to have a father." She wiped her eyes with the back of her hand.

Phillipe offered her his handkerchief. Annie dabbed her tears but could no longer stop the flow of her words. "Then she met Dan and we both believed this time it really would be different. He *did* marry her. He even bought us a trailer, and for a while we were like a real family. But right after Rick was born Dan vanished into thin air just like the others. Later we found out he'd been married to someone else all along." Annie shook her head. "Mom couldn't handle the pain of that last rejection. She began to drink. She died six years ago. Rick and I still live in the trailer."

Hot tears trickled down Annie's face as she finished speaking. For a moment Phillipe stared at her. "I'm not like those men," he said finally. "I won't abandon you."

Her chest rose and fell heavily. She stared directly into his eyes. "Don't you think the men in my mother's life fed her the same line?"

He drew in a slow breath. "Would it make you feel better if I had my attorney draw up a binding contract?"

"Why? To ease your conscience?"

He never flinched from the scathing sarcasm of her tone nor lowered his eyes from hers. "Why are you denying me the chance to compromise?"

Annie made no reply. Instead, she closed her eyes, blinking back stinging tears. Of all the men on the face of the earth, why did she have to fall so hopelessly in love with this one? And why couldn't he love her in return? He probably took pity on her. To him she was a poor, unfortunate woman who had stumbled into his life and served as a temporary distraction. Nothing more. She wasn't worth his commitment.

For several minutes she tried to swallow the massive lump in her throat. Taking a deep breath, she steeled her resolution. Slowly raising her eyes to his, she said, "I think it's time for me to leave, Phillipe."

He was staring at her disbelievingly. "I think you're making a big mistake."

She stiffened at his words. "The only mistake I made

was getting to know you," she murmured. "It's been an experience I'll never forget." She turned away. With torment and sadness propelling her unsteady legs, she walked to her cabin.

Chapter Eleven

Annie rested her head against the window and closed her eyes. She listened to the *whirr* of the plane's engines and felt the air pressure change with lift-off. It was over.

Fatigue enveloped her and she stretched her legs as best she could, allowing her tense muscles to relax. She opened her eyes and looked down, staring at the sparkling water below, watching the miles fly by. Her face grew moist with tears.

She thought about going home. It felt as if she'd been gone a month instead of just seven days. So much had changed and so much was the same. She would still live in her small trailer, still work twelve-hour shifts at Sadie's Place, and still have to pay the bills. However, now she had more financial security. More choices. After Rick graduated, maybe she'd sell the trailer and move to Des Moines, go to college. Nothing was anchoring her to Parker Junction. There were better places, as Phillipe had pointed out.

He was right about a lot of things. He'd shown her how much more there was to life than she'd ever dreamed possible. He'd also broken her heart and left her with a feeling of utter emptiness.

After returning to her cabin the night before, she'd never cried for so long. She had been a fool. A complete fool. She could accept that. But why couldn't she shake the feeling of shame?

One part of her almost regretted meeting him, while the other held dear each and every second they had spent together. Would the memories sustain her for a lifetime?

The following week was, without a doubt, one of the worst Annie could remember. To add to her misery, upon returning home, she discovered that Rick had moved into an apartment with another student. He'd taken their television, microwave, and dishes. He'd left the utility bill, tuition statement, and a can of soup.

Two of the part-time waitresses had the flu, so Annie worked double shifts. She welcomed the distraction. Sadie had a date with a mechanic and she closed the diner at noon on New Year's Eve. Annie spent the evening alone in her trailer.

It wasn't getting any easier. The harder she tried to keep Phillipe out of her thoughts, the more impossible it was not to think of him. She finally gave up on the book she was reading, pulled on her boots, and went for a walk in the snow.

At work the next day, she forced a smile on her face. Her tanned skin and sunny glow convinced the casual observer that all was right in her world. Sadie, however, wasn't easily fooled. She'd tried unsuccessfully to wheedle information from Annie every day since she'd returned. Today was no different.

As they stood shoulder-to-shoulder inserting new menus into the green plastic holders, Annie tried humming to avoid conversation. When she realized she was humming one of Phillipe's recent releases, she swallowed down the rest of the melody.

"You don't seem as rested as I expected. I suspect you probably stayed up till the wee hours every mornin' just dancin' your feet off with some rich businessman," Sadie chided.

Annie shook her head.

"What's that supposed to mean?" Sadie's voice was brisk with impatience. "Didn't you dance, or didn't you meet any rich businessmen?" She followed Annie to the coffee maker.

"I danced with the cruise director," Annie supplied, "and a few other men, but I don't remember any of their names."

Sadie threw her hands into the air. "From the look on your face I'd guess you just got back from a funeral instead of a vacation. Land's sake, girl, didn't you do anything fun?" After a pause that Annie made no effort to fill, Sadie shrugged and began to pour salt into shakers. "I know something's itchin' at you, and it ain't got nothin' to do with Rick movin' out. When you're ready to tell me, I'll have my ears on."

Annie gave her boss a weak smile and finished making coffee. It was the middle of the afternoon, the slowest and worst part of the day. She'd just started to wrap silverware when the door swung open and Gus hurried in.

"Happy New Year, ladies!"

Annie and Sadie returned the greeting in unison.

"What brings you here on a holiday, old man?" Sadie wanted to know.

Gus shrugged off his coat and slid into a booth. "The power's off at my house. The ice storm this morning brought down some limbs and it looks like it'll take most of the day to replace the power lines."

"What next?" Sadie wailed. "I thought with the snow and all we'd have a slow day. Elmo, start makin' a batch of chili. Folks'll be swarmin' in here tryin' to keep warm. Annie, bring Gus a cup of coffee and smile at him real pretty. Maybe he'll offer to wrap napkins around a few forks while you help me in the kitchen."

"Go ahead and put me to work," Gus said to Annie as she set a cup of coffee in front of him. "Say, where'd you get that fancy pin? Was that one of your prizes?"

Annie felt a blush rise on her cheeks. She shook her head. "It was a . . . a Christmas gift."

"A Christmas gift!" Sadie repeated as if she couldn't believe her ears. She scurried across the diner. "Who in tarnation gave you that?"

"A man I met on the ship," Annie returned.

Sadie gasped and clutched her hand to her heart. "You mean to tell me that you've been mopin' around here actin' like nothin' special happened when all the while some man got you a hunk of jewelry with enough ice on it to fill a skating rink?"

"Are those real diamonds?" Gus asked, squinting his eyes to get a better look. Annie nodded.

Sadie took hold of her elbow. "Do you remember the name of the man who bought it?"

She might as well get it over with and supply Sadie with enough information to satisfy her curiosity, Annie decided. She knew her boss well enough to know that the hounding and cross-examining would continue unabated. "Phillipe Nadeau bought the pin for me," Annie said, struggling to keep her tone light. It surprised her that she could say his name in such a normal voice.

"Phillipe Nadeau!" Sadie shrieked.

"The singer?" Gus asked at the same time.

"That's right," Annie replied.

"I can't believe it," Sadie said to Gus. "She actually met Phillipe Nadeau. I've got goose bumps on my arms just thinkin' about him." She shoved up her sleeve to prove her reaction. "Is that rascal as handsome in person as he is on television?"

"Much, much more," Annie admitted. Tears were suddenly close to the surface, threatening to clog her throat. She wanted to end this conversation as quickly as possible.

Sadie, however, wasn't about to let the matter rest. "He didn't pass out jewelry to all the women, did he?"

"Not that I'm aware of," Annie answered.

Elmo came out of the kitchen and stood in front of her, hands on his hips. "Why did he pick you out of the crowd?" he asked.

"I wish I knew," Annie mumbled. "Sadie, would you like me to make a pot of hot chocolate?"

Sadie gave her a long, measuring look and shook her head. "You've always been such a reliable, sensible, practical woman. Tell me you haven't lost your head to a man like Phillipe Nadeau." *Typical Sadie,*

Annie thought. She always cut straight to the heart of the matter.

"My head's sitting squarely on my shoulders, Sadie," she said firmly.

Two customers walked in and Annie met them at their table with the coffeepot. She was more than thankful for the diversion. She took their orders and passed Sadie on the way to the pickup window.

"It just doesn't make any sense. Why would he buy you a pin like that? I don't understand what's gotten into men these days," Sadie commiserated before moving on to another table of customers.

She didn't understand what had gotten into men either, Annie thought. When they got too close to a woman, and the next logical step was commitment, they panicked and left. Love, apparently, was a frightening thing to men.

An hour later Annie was balancing a tray with three bowls of chili, a basket of crackers, two salads, and an order of onion rings when she heard Elmo emit a low whistle.

Suddenly the noise in the diner faded to a few hushed whispers. Annie felt a strange sensation sweep over her, one she hadn't felt for over a week. She sat the tray onto the counter before turning around—in time to see a man brushing snow from his shoulders as the door closed behind him.

When she saw him striding across the room toward her, she froze. For a fraction of an instant her knees became so wobbly she felt as if she were back on the waves in the Caribbean. She gripped the counter, bracing herself.

It couldn't be him. He belonged in her fantasy world, not here in the diner.

As he came closer, Annie told herself her eyes were playing tricks on her. It was only the snow reflecting in through the windows; an illusion created by an overactive imagination. It had happened several times before during the past week. She'd catch a glimpse of someone tall, with dark, wavy hair and a special smile, and she'd experience this same feeling of light-headedness. Then she'd discover some stranger standing there, watching her as if she'd lost her mind.

But this time there was no mistake. It was Phillipe. Fighting off a wave of dizziness, she tried to remain outwardly calm. Her insides were quivering like gelatin.

Phillipe looked better than she'd remembered, if that was possible. He was dressed exactly as he'd been the last time she'd seen him, wearing a black dinner jacket, a faintly ruffled shirt above trim black slacks, and— Wait a minute! Annie's mind changed channels mid-thought. Why would he wear a tuxedo in the middle of the afternoon in a snowstorm? He wasn't even wearing a topcoat. It didn't make sense. Nothing made sense.

He stepped closer and Annie noticed his bow tie was gone and his pleated shirt looked as if he'd slept in it. His hair was mussed and a day's growth of beard darkened his cheeks.

He paused just in front of her. His eyes held hers with the same intensity she remembered from that very first day.

Annie stopped breathing. They stared at each other.

She felt the blood drain from her face and wondered if she was about to faint again.

"Hello, Anna."

His voice was the same molasses-smooth ripple she remembered so well. "Hello, Phillipe," she returned with much more calmness and poise than she felt.

His eyes searched hers. "I'm so glad I finally found you."

Why had he been looking for her? she wondered, staring into his slightly bloodshot eyes.

"What are you doing here?" This time her voice came out weak and hollow.

"I came to see you."

Flustered to the tips of her white tennis shoes, Annie lowered her gaze and was even more frazzled when she spotted chili stains on the front of her uniform. Why had he come here? Why did he have to see her like this?

"How did you find me?" she asked.

Phillipe gave a low chuckle. "You'd never believe it."

"Oh?"

He nodded. "I finished performing in Vegas just after midnight. Then I chartered a plane to Des Moines. The airport was closed because of the bad weather so I flew to Omaha, rented a car, and drove two hundred miles through a blinding snowstorm." He paused, then asked, "Why don't you have a phone?"

Annie stared at him. She didn't want to tell him why she didn't have a phone. She didn't want to tell him anything. She tried to swallow the awful lump in her throat. "Would you like a cup of coffee and a menu?"

"I didn't come here to eat. I want to talk with you," he said, his expression held in tight check.

Her heart pulsed. "I'm on duty. I don't have time—"

"Listen to what the man has to say," Sadie said, picking up Annie's tray. "I'll cover your tables."

"Is she your boss?" Phillipe asked.

Annie nodded.

"Sadie," he called, then smiled his most charming smile. "Is there somewhere Anna and I can talk privately?"

Sadie set the tray onto a table and smoothed her springy red curls before returning his smile. "You two could go into the storage room, behind the kitchen. Annie, have Elmo give you the key."

"Wait a minute!" Annie insisted. "I have no intention—"

"I think you will when you hear what I have to say."

She flushed furiously when she realized all eyes and ears were trained on her. "Phillipe," she whispered in a low, firm voice, "anything you have to say to me can be said right here." She tapped her finger on the counter for emphasis. Heaven help her if she had to be alone with him!

"Well, the decision is yours, but I think you'd be more comfortable talking privately."

"We'll talk here," she repeated, feeling anything but comfortable.

"All right, if you say so." At Annie's nod, he continued. "Before I left the ship, I took inventory of all my possessions and I discovered something valuable

was missing.'' She heard several people gasp. ''I have
every reason to believe you took it.''

Annie sucked in her breath. ''You think I'm a
thief?'' She met Phillipe's gaze and felt a feeling of
despair wash over her. A muscle in his face started to
twitch, but he said nothing. It had to be a mistake. He
must have misplaced whatever it was he accused her
of stealing. Her head began to throb and her palms
became clammy. As upset as she was, she knew she
had to say something in her own defense. She swallowed, then said, ''I have never stolen anything in my
entire life.''

Gus walked quickly over to her side. ''I can vouch
for this woman, Mr. Nadeau. I've known her since she
was a baby, and she's one of the most honest people
you'd ever want to meet.'' His voice could barely be
heard above the murmurs of the crowd.

When Phillipe spoke again, the room fell silent.
''I'm not doubting her honesty, Mr.—''

''Sanders,'' Gus supplied, while shaking Phillipe's
extended hand. ''Gus Sanders.''

''Gus, in all fairness to Anna, I must say that she
had every reason to believe the item she took was hers
for the taking.''

''I didn't take—'' Annie began.

Sadie cut her off. ''Hush up, girl, and let the man
say his piece.'' She gestured to a pair of customers.
''Bill, you and Slim take seats over there at the counter
so Annie and Mr. Nadeau can sit here at this table and
talk things out.'' The pair of burly truckers nodded in
agreement and smiled sheepishly at Annie as they

picked up their mugs and backed over to a pair of stools.

"Go over there and sit down, Annie," Sadie said, tugging on her employee's sleeve. "Let's try to settle this sensibly without involving the police."

"The police!" Annie exclaimed. "Now, wait just a—"

"We won't need to call the police, Sadie. This is a personal matter between Anna and me," Annie heard Phillipe say as she moved with hesitant steps around the circular counter. There must be fifty customers in the diner, she realized, and every one of them had turned in his seat to watch the show. She felt miserable. Humiliated and miserable.

Annie sank onto one of the worn aluminum-and-vinyl chairs, a far cry from the plush dining-room seats on the cruise ship, she thought. Taking a deep, steadying breath, she lifted her eyes to Phillipe. For a heart-stopping moment he stared at her, searching her soul for something known only to him. When she broke the contact with a blink, he sat down in the other chair. He immediately placed his elbows on the table and lowered his chin into his hands.

He looked as tired and frazzled as Annie felt. Good, she thought with satisfaction. If he was heartless enough to intrude into her world, stomp on her heart, and call her a thief, then he deserved to feel wretched.

Sadie stuck her order book into her apron pocket and placed her hands on her hips. "Now, what's this all about? Are you accusin' Annie of stealin' that pin?" She pointed to the bejeweled butterfly.

Customers stood and strained their necks to get a better look. Annie's face turned crimson.

"No," Phillipe assured her. "The pin was a gift." He smiled at Annie. "I'm pleased you're wearing it."

Annie looked squarely at Phillipe. "Is it the money? Did you have second thoughts about the money?"

"You stole money?" Elmo asked, his voice rising to the rafters.

"No!" Annie and Phillipe said in unison.

Phillipe rose abruptly. "Sadie, it's imperative that Anna and I talk privately, so if you'll all excuse us. . . ." He offered his hand to Annie.

She stood but refused to touch him. "Follow me," she called over her shoulder. Elmo raced ahead and unlocked a heavy metal door covered with peeling paint.

Annie flipped on the light switch, illuminating a small room lined with boxes. Phillipe followed her in and she closed the door behind them. She narrowed her eyes and tried to look as menacing as possible. "You certainly have my attention now," she said. "What is it you're accusing me of stealing?"

Phillipe sighed softly and took a half step back from her. His gaze held hers. It wasn't an annoyed, indignant expression registering in his eyes, but something softer. If Annie didn't know better, she'd swear. . . . No, that was ridiculous.

They stood face-to-face for several seconds, each absorbed with the other. Finally, Phillipe reached for Annie's hand. He lifted her palm to his chest and placed it on his shirt.

"What do you feel, Anna?" he murmured.

"Feel?" she repeated. "I don't feel anything."

He raised her hand and brought it to his lips. Annie stood mesmerized as he kissed it and returned it to his chest. "You can't feel anything, because there's nothing there." He released her hand and drew a deep breath. "When I watched you get off the ship last week, I realized you took my heart with you."

His heart? She had stolen his heart? Annie felt a tear fall from her eye. "Phillipe—"

"I was wrong. I was a coward and a fool to let you walk away from me," he said, his voice oddly hoarse.

She blushed, a scorching, scarlet stain right up to her ears. "You've had my heart since the first minute I saw you, Phillipe, but I still won't live with you."

"That's good," he said resolutely, "because I'm withdrawing my invitation."

Annie looked up at him, uncomprehending. She didn't trust her voice but knew he was waiting for her to say something. She took a step sideways, trying to put a little distance between them. "The week I spent on the ship was the best week of my entire life. I never wanted it to end." She sighed heavily. "But it did end. I can't go on living in a fantasy world."

"Why?"

Annie swallowed. "You, of all people, should know why," she answered, her voice shaking with emotion.

"Anna, do you love me?"

"Yes," she whispered without hesitation.

"And I love you with all my heart and soul." He caught a tear with the tip of his finger as it rolled down her cheek. "You taught me to listen to my heart and not be afraid of becoming emotionally bound to someone.'' He slid his fingers through her hair and tilted her head to face his. ''I want to show you the world, Anna. I want to take you on the Orient Express, to Paris, Rome, Athens. . . .'' His voice choked with emotion. ''If you say you'll marry me, you'll make me the happiest man in the world.''

''He wants to marry her!'' Elmo announced through the door in a voice loud enough to be heard on the interstate. Applause erupted in the diner like the thunderous roar of firecrackers on the Fourth of July.

Annie brought her mouth to his and whispered against his lips. ''Consider yourself a happy man, Phillipe.'' His arms wrapped around her tightly.

Just then, the door burst open and Sadie rushed in. ''Did Elmo hear right? Are you two gettin' married?''

''Elmo heard right,'' Phillipe confirmed, his eyes never straying from Annie's.

''Then what are you doin' back here in the storeroom?'' Sadie said, taking each of them by an elbow. ''I've got a restaurant full of customers waitin' to congratulate you.''

''I think we're about to make a public announcement,'' Annie said as they stepped into the room.

Phillipe grinned, brushing her freckled nose with the tip of his finger. ''How do you feel about getting married tonight in Las Vegas?''

Annie's eyes widened. ''Tonight? Las Vegas?''

''That is if you think we could get some people to volunteer to act as our witnesses on such short notice.'' He turned to Sadie and Gus. ''Would you do us the honor? I'll charter a plane.''

Gus nodded eagerly. Sadie swished over to a sign

hanging on the door and flipped it over to read CLOSED. She peered out the window, then turned to her customers. ''The weather's let up. All of you clear out of here!''

Amid the laughter, whistles, and cheers, Phillipe gathered Annie into his arms. She ran her hands lovingly over his shoulders. Soon she would be his, and he hers. Forever. She squeezed her eyes shut and smiled a secret smile.

Annie Stewart always knew that if she wished upon a star, her dreams really would come true.